COLD-BL[OODED]

Deputy Marshal Vince Pendergast marched into the saloon and the congenial mood evaporated like mist in the sun. This was not entirely surprising to Longarm for he had experienced the same effect when he had often entered a saloon in search of a fugitive. Longarm could feel the sudden tension as Vince leaned over the bar and whispered something to the bartender, who motioned him toward a back room.

Longarm's interest was piqued, but he did not think much about Vince, and about ten minutes passed before the deputy marshal appeared again. Suddenly, Vince drew his six-gun, pivoted on one heel and fired one of the fastest, smoothest draws Longarm had ever witnessed.

At the end of the bar, a tall, thick-chested man cried out as he tried to drag up his own gun. Vince fired two more times, each of his bullets striking the man in the chest and knocking him back a step until he crashed over a spittoon.

Vince then walked over to the dead man and brazenly emptied his pockets of a thick roll of cash, the rings from his fingers and even his gold pocket watch. When he straightened, Vince said to no one in particular, "This man's name was Earl Jessup and he was wanted in Tucson for murder. I gave him what he deserved. Anyone have a problem with that?"

No one, including Longarm, said a word.

TABOR EVANS

LONGARM

AND THE
MYSTERIOUS MISTRESS

JOVE BOOKS, NEW YORK

LONGARM AND THE MYSTERIOUS MISTRESS

A Jove Book / published by arrangement with
the author

PRINTING HISTORY
Jove edition / August 2002

Copyright © 2002 by Penguin Putnam Inc.

Visit our website at
www.penguinputnam.com

ISBN: 0-515-13351-5

A JOVE BOOK®
Jove Books are published by The Berkley Publishing Group,
a division of Penguin Putnam Inc.,
375 Hudson Street, New York, New York 10014.
JOVE and the "J" design
are trademarks belonging to Penguin Putnam Inc.

Chapter 1

It was a fine October morning in Denver, and Longarm was enjoying himself as he strolled arm and arm along Cherry Creek with Mattie McGuire, his latest love. She was tall like he was, and they made a striking couple as they walked along the winding path through the trees with the nearby rain-swollen creek.

"I'm so glad that you're not going to have to go off on another assignment for at least a month," Mattie said, looking up into Custis Long's blue-gray eyes. "It's seems like every time there's something really difficult for your office to handle, they send you off again!"

"I know," Longarm replied, "but, in a way, it's also flattering. I mean, imagine how I'd feel if my boss, Billy Vail, chose someone else whenever a tough job was at hand?"

"But you've proven yourself a hundred times!" Mattie protested, her rosebud lips forming a pout. "Why can't they find someone else to help share the load and risk their life? My goodness, darling, you've been shot, stabbed and left for dead in the most godforsaken places! One of these days. . . ."

Longarm stopped, turned and lifted her chin. "Dear

1

Mattie, will you please stop worrying about me so much? I'm perfectly capable of taking care of myself, and I actually enjoy . . ."

"Help!"

Longarm whirled to the cry, his hand snaking across his waist for the Colt revolver that he wore on his left hip, butt facing forward.

"Where are you?" he shouted.

"I'm drowning! Someone please help!"

Through a gap in the trees and willows, Longarm could see Cherry Creek swiftly flowing. Without hesitation, he broke into a hard run, batting bushes and shrubbery aside as he made his way through the thickets to the edge of the water. And then, he saw a small boy being swept along by the snow-fed runoff. Tearing off his coat and gunbelt, then pulling off his boots, Longarm ran into the water and waded in until the current was waist high. It was so cold it took his breath away. The boy was already twenty yards downstream so Longarm dove into the torrent and swam hard, ignoring the cold and hoping he could reach the kid before he went under for the last time.

"Hang on!" he shouted, racing with the current as they were swept under a bridge, causing the sun to disappear. In the frigid cold and darkness, he yelled, "Hang on!"

When they passed back out into sunlight, Longarm heard people shouting encouragement from up on the bridge, but his full attention was on the boy who was now being carried around a bend and sent into a chute where Longarm well knew the water was especially treacherous.

The boy disappeared in the churning, rain-fed creek. Swimming with all of his considerable strength, Longarm shot forward until he reached the spot where the child had vanished, and then he took several more strokes before he dove into the muddy torrent.

There was no visibility, and while blindly searching for the boy Longarm crashed into a submerged boulder. The

2

force of impact was so strong and unexpected that the air was pounded from his already burning lungs. Terror filled his mind, and Longarm lost track of which direction was up and which was down. Lungs ready to burst for the need of fresh air, he clawed at the water, praying that he'd not strike another submerged boulder, which would surely kill him.

While grappling wildly and straining to find the surface and life-giving oxygen, his fingers hooked on to what he immediately recognized as clothing, and then he felt the boy's limp body. Longarm's strong fingers closed like a trap and, with his free arm and long legs, he continued to swim knowing he had only seconds left to get air or he was finished.

When at last he broke the surface, Longarm whooped as he sucked in fresh air. Then he spotted the closest point of the shore and swam with all of his waning strength. With the unconscious boy in tow, it seemed as if he were dragging a ton of bricks that wanted to pull him down to a watery grave.

Along the bank of Cherry Creek, frantic bystanders waded into the water and reached out to help the fading United States marshal. But the current was so unrelenting that it carried Longarm and the boy almost another mile before they collided with a fallen and partially submerged cottonwood. Suddenly, they were enmeshed in its tangle of branches, one of which impaled Longarm like a spear, causing him to almost lose consciousness.

"Hang on!" someone cried.

Longarm was trying, but his strength was gone. The underwater collision with the boulder, the terrible temperature of the snow-fed water, and now the added trauma of being impaled by a sharp tree limb was more than even he could endure and he lost consciousness.

• • •

3

Longarm awakened hearing voices, and when he opened his eyes, he saw a silver-haired man peering intently at him through thick lenses that made his pale blue eyes appear abnormally large. "Who are you?" he asked, feeling weak and disoriented.

"I'm Dr. Cutler," the man said, as a white-uniformed nurse moved away.

With a sudden jolt, he remembered his ordeal in Cherry Creek. "What about the boy I dove into the water after?"

"I'm pleased to say that he's made a complete recovery," Cutler said. "We discharged him from this hospital after a short observation period. Other than some cuts and bruises, young Donald Hamilton is in excellent shape. I wish we could say the same thing for you, Marshal Long."

Longarm shook his head and tried to sit up, but the effort caused him to feel as if he'd been lanced. The pain was so intense that he had to bite his lower lip to keep from crying out.

"Don't even try to move," the doctor ordered. "We've had to dig pieces of rotting wood out of your gut, and we're just hoping that none of your internal organs have been pierced and that infection doesn't invade your abdominal cavity."

Longarm gazed down at the white sheet covering his chest, then looked back at Dr. Cutler. "How long have I been unconscious?"

"Two days. You were hemorrhaging very badly and in shock when they rushed you here in a buckboard wagon. We all thought you were a goner, but your strength and youth pulled you through."

"Doc, I'm no youth."

Cutler frowned and said, "I meant that, if you had been old and in poor physical shape, you'd most likely have died on the operating-room table."

Longarm turned his head from one side to the other. *Yes, this is definitely a hospital room, with its pale and*

4

unadorned walls and the strong smell of disinfectant. "Look, Doc. I hate hospitals, so how soon can I get out of here?"

"You're running a low-grade but persistent fever, and your pulse is still erratic. So I'd estimate you'll be here for at least two weeks . . . if your recovery progresses as we hope and expect."

But Longarm shook his head. "Doc, I'm not lying in a bed for two weeks. I've got things to do!" He was going to say more, but was unexpectedly seized by a fit of hard coughing.

When his deep wracking cough finally subsided, the doctor reached for his stethoscope, saying, "Marshal, take a deep breath, then expel your lungs slowly."

"But . . ."

"Just do as I say!"

The physician listened to his breathing, and even Longarm could tell his lungs were filled with congestion. The doctor reached over to the bedside table and grabbed a tin cup. Holding it before Longarm's mouth, he said, "Try to cough it up."

Longarm coughed hard, and then he filled the tin cup with yellowish-colored phlegm.

When the doctor placed the tin cup on a bedside table and turned back to him, Longarm said, "That looks like pretty bad stuff I spat up just now."

"You are quite ill, Marshal," the doctor replied. "Pneumonia is a killer. Now, keep breathing in and out as deeply as possible."

Longarm realized that he was having trouble getting his breath and that his lungs ached. He'd seen plenty of strong men suddenly afflicted with pneumonia, and he knew it was nothing to take lightly.

"Marshal, you are a brave man, but you've damaged your lungs to a degree where they might never fully recover," Cutler finally told him in a solemn voice.

"Cherry Creek was real cold and muddy. I had a hard time getting to the kid."

"So we've been told. You are quite the hero right now."

"I don't give a damn about that."

"I believe you, but since heroes are rare, everyone in town is filled with gratitude for your extraordinary act of heroism. The mayor, even the governor, have all sent you congratulations and their wishes for a speedy recovery."

"That's nice, but I'd far rather have a good set of lungs."

Dr. Cutler pulled back Longarm's bedsheet and then gently lifted the bandages fixed to his side. Longarm studied the man's face as he examined the puncture wound.

"Well, Doc? Am I going to survive?"

"We certainly hope that's the case. If you can hold off an acute abdominal-cavity infection which we call a peritonitis, then we'll have to fully address the pneumonia."

"How soon will you know about my gut?"

"If your fever doesn't rise any more within the next twenty-four hours, I feel confident that you're not going to succumb to peritonitis."

"Twenty-four hours?"

"That's right."

"What are my chances?"

"Good, I'd say. We think we were able to clean and then sterilize the wound. We sutured you back up, and, right now at least, it looks clean."

"All right," Longarm said, feeling very warm and a little dizzy. "Doc, I'm going to make it. I've been shot and stabbed, and I always bounce back sooner than anyone expects."

"I'm glad to hear that," Cutler replied. "But as far as I'm concerned, pneumonia is the real problem standing in your road to recovery."

"What can I do to beat it?"

"The prescription is always the same . . . dry heat and

6

sunshine in addition to a good deal of rest. Denver winters are hard, and you need a warmer climate. The thing about pneumonia is that it is pernicious."

"What's that mean?"

"It means that it hangs on, and quite often, just when the patient thinks he or she is recovered, they take a deadly turn for the worse. So, rest and hot, dry air is the best medicine."

"Doc, what are you suggesting?"

"I'm suggesting that you need a long period of convalescence in a winter climate that is very warm and dry . . . as it is in Arizona."

"But . . ."

"You have a couple of visitors," Cutler said, obviously terminating the conversation. "I'll give each of them just five minutes. The most important thing now is that you rest and keep trying to cough up the phlegm so that we can keep your lungs from filling, which would cause you to suffocate."

"I'll do my best here, but I sure don't like rest or quiet," Longarm snapped. "I quickly become bored."

Cutler gazed thoughtfully at him, eyebrows knitted downward in disapproval. He drew a pen from his white smock and then found a pad of paper and scribbled something that he put back in his pocket.

Finally, he said, "Mr. Vail told me to expect that you would be a difficult and unwilling patient. And I assured your supervisor that your choice was very clear . . . either do as you are ordered for the sake of your health . . . or you die either of peritonitis or pneumonia, which I believe can evolve into tuberculosis."

Longarm's eyes opened wide, and his mouth went dry with fear. "Well," he said quietly, "I guess I'll just have to take your orders and try to get healthy again. I sure don't want to become a tubercular and wind up like poor old Doc Holiday, or like some others I've seen coughing blood."

"Good," Cutler told him. "Now, I'm going to allow Miss McGuire in for a very short visit. Just don't let the young woman excite you."

Longarm managed a smile. "She can do it."

"So I gathered. The poor young woman was hysterical when you arrived, and she hovered about here until we sent her home to get some desperately needed sleep. Anyway, I insist that you keep her visit short and do not become excited or you will have another bad spell of coughing."

"But I thought I was supposed to cough to clear my lungs."

"You are, Marshal, but only with a nurse or myself in attendance. If you cough too hard, you can rupture blood vessels in your lungs and hemorrhage to death."

"I see. I need to cough, but not too hard."

"Exactly so. Now, I'm allowing the young woman five minutes at your bedside, but not a moment longer. Then, if you feel up to it, we'll allow your supervisor the same amount of time."

"I'll be up to it."

"We shall see," the doctor intoned with a solemn note in his voice. "I'll have a nurse watch you closely, and she will terminate the visits if you exhibit any signs of distress. Is that agreeable?"

Having no choice in the matter and now convinced of the seriousness of his condition, Longarm nodded. "Whatever you say, Doc."

Cutler left his bedside and was soon replaced by Mattie. When she leaned over and kissed his lips, the poor woman burst into sobs and hugged him so tightly that Longarm almost suffocated.

"Mattie," he pleaded, pushing her away and gasping for breath. "Take it easy!"

"Yes," she said, trying to regain her composure. "I'm sorry! It's just that I've been so upset. Everyone wants to see and congratulate you for saving that dear boy. You're a hero, and they even wrote up what happened on the front page of the newspaper."

"That's nice," Longarm told the woman as she dabbed at her leaking eyes. "But all I want is to rest and take it easy for a while. The doctor says that . . . if I don't die of a stomach infection . . . I need to go to Arizona for the winter just as soon as I'm strong enough to travel."

"I know. He told me and Mr. Vail that this high altitude and a hard winter could wreck your recovery."

"Then I'd better visit the low desert country," Longarm told her.

She squeezed his hand and gazed into his eyes. "Custis, I want to go to Arizona with you."

"Mattie, thanks, but that's not necessary. You have a good job here and . . ."

"I can find another job waitressing anywhere. Darling, you're what's important."

Longarm was touched. "Mattie, you're very special. I could use your help."

"Then let's talk no more about it," she said brightly. "I'll quit my job when it's time to leave here, and we'll just get on the train and see Arizona. It'll be good for you and a real adventure for me. I've never even been out of Colorado."

"Well, Mattie," Longarm said, suddenly realizing that he was not really sure that he wanted to be with this sweet but scatterbrained woman on a full-time basis. "I'm not at all sure that you'd like Arizona."

"Why not?"

"Because down in Arizona they have rattlesnakes, tarantulas, Gila monsters and scorpions . . ."

Her jaw dropped. "They have all those horrible creatures?"

9

"I'm afraid so. And it's nearly impossible to keep scorpions out of your bed at night. They have these poison-stingers that coil over their backs."

"Oh no!"

"I just thought I ought to tell you the truth, Mattie. And, I suppose I also should mention the Apache."

"What about them?"

Longarm shrugged. "It's just that they never really surrendered. And, unfortunately, they still catch and scalp whites."

"No!"

"It is pretty awful," Longarm said. "They have a massacre down there every week or two."

Mattie gulped and tried to smile. "Custis, maybe I should come down and join you later. I mean, I don't have any money saved, and, well . . . I need to think this over a little bit before I quit my job."

"Yeah, you do like your job."

"That's right. So if you don't mind, I think you should go ahead, and then I'll probably follow."

"That might be a good idea," Longarm agreed, trying to look disappointed. "You're a Denver girl, and I don't think you'd do well in the desert."

"Oh, thank you," Mattie said with obvious relief. "That's one of the things I love about you, Custis. You are always so reasonable."

"Yes."

A nurse appeared. "Time is up, Miss McGuire."

Mattie kissed him on the cheek. "I'll be back soon," she promised as she was ushered out of his room.

Longarm shook his head. He liked Mattie a great deal, but she talked his head off, and she'd have driven him crazy if she'd accompanied him to Arizona.

"Well, hello there!" Billy Vail practically shouted as he burst into the room bearing a large bouquet of flowers. "How you doin', hero?"

10

"Don't call me that."

"Why not? You're the talk of the town! Why, our director is planning to honor you with a special ceremony and a medal . . . or certificate or whatever we can come up with that doesn't bust the coffee fund."

"That's great," Longarm told his boss without enthusiasm. He would have said more but he was suddenly seized by a fit of hard coughing. Longarm pointed to the tin cup and Billy finally understood.

"Holy cow," Billy exclaimed a few minutes later. "You've got some bad-looking stuff in your lungs! No wonder Dr. Cutler is insisting that, if you survive the stomach thing, you need to take time off and go to recuperate in Arizona."

The coughing and spitting up of phlegm had left him light-headed and dizzy again. "I'll survive and make a full recovery," he managed to reply. "Just keep my job open until I get back."

"You're irreplaceable, and I've already cleared it with Mr. Pullman. He says you can go on sick leave at half your pay for as long as it takes for you to recover."

"Half pay!"

Billy shrugged. "You know that we're short of money and always falling short of our budget."

"But, dammit, Billy, how am I going to survive in Arizona on a lousy thirty-five dollars a month!"

"Don't you have any savings in the bank?"

"Are you kidding?"

Billy frowned. "Hmmm. I expect not, huh?"

"That's right. So tell Mr. Pullman that I'll be back in harness by fall and that, until then, I expect *full pay*."

Billy looked nervous. "I'll see what I can do. You know I'll be pulling for you, Custis. And, if we can't come through with full pay, we'll pass the hat in the office. You know, take up a collection."

"Don't do that," Longarm growled. "Just get me a

ticket to Arizona and full pay until I return in the fall."

"You want the government to *pay* for your train ticket?"

"Yes, dammit!"

Billy sighed. "You're asking the world, Custis. But I'll do what I can for you. You know that I will."

After that, he and Billy didn't have a lot to say to each other, and it was almost a relief when the nurse poked her head in the door and told Billy that his time was up and he needed to leave.

Chapter 2

Longarm was not a model hospital patient. And although he felt feverish the first few days of his recovery, by the end of the week he was well on the mend and completely bored and restless.

"You just have to learn to take it easy," Mattie told him one afternoon. "Why, you act as if you were ready to go fight the world."

"I feel as though I could whip a wildcat," he groused. "And to tell you the truth, I'm fed up with this hospital. The food is terrible and most of the nurses are a bunch of frustrated generals always telling me what I can or can't do."

"What did Dr. Cutler say when he looked at you this morning?"

"He said that my wound is healing fine, and I'm not going to die of peritonitis."

"And about your lungs?"

Longarm scowled. "He said they're still filled with phlegm and that it'll take months for them to clear completely unless I go to Arizona where the air is drier and more healthful."

"How soon can you leave?"

"Next week," Longarm said. "But I really can't afford to take the time off if I'm only being paid at half my normal wages."

"I thought Mr. Vail was working on that."

"He is," Longarm answered. "And I'm hoping he can get it taken care of in the next day or two. I don't want to have to go to the desert and live in an Indian's wickiup or a run-down shack."

"Of course you don't, poor thing! And I'm sorry you're so restless and unhappy."

Longarm reached for Mattie's hand and said, "You could help me out a little."

Her large blue eyes widened with surprise. "Me?"

"Sure," he said, brushing his fingers over her ample bosom. "We could lock the door and relieve our tensions in less than fifteen minutes of lovemaking."

"Custis," she whispered, looking astonished by his suggestion. "This *is* a hospital!"

"You don't have to remind me. Go close and lock the door. The doctors and nurses have already taken their morning rounds, and they probably won't even notice that my door is shut."

"But what if they do?"

"Too bad," Longarm said, starting to unbutton the front of her dress.

"Stop that!" Mattie protested, jumping away from the bed. "Are you crazy? What if we got too excited and that wound of yours was torn open or you started coughing yourself to death?"

"Then at least I'd die a happy man," he replied. "I don't need any more medicine or nursing. What I need is *you!*"

"Custis, you're a very sick man," she scolded. "I think you must be slightly delirious even to suggest such an outrageous thing like that in the middle of a hospital."

"Ten minutes," he said, hating the pleading in his voice. "They'll never have a clue."

Mattie came back over to stand beside his bed. "If something happened to you while we were making love . . . I'd never forgive myself. I'd be haunted with guilt for the rest of my life. I'd be responsible for your death!"

"What I'm dying for you alone can provide," Longarm told the pretty young woman. "Isn't it the least you can do for a hero?"

"Custis, you're awful. And besides, I don't think you're in any condition to do what you're proposing."

He pulled back his bedsheet and blanket to show her that he was not only willing, but ready and able to make love. "The truth is, Mattie, you can't keep a good man's organ down."

"Why, you're absolutely shameless!" Mattie cried, but she was smiling.

"Close and lock the door."

She pursed her lips and studied his face. "Five minutes," she said, "and we do it *gently.*"

Longarm grinned wolfishly. "It's a deal."

Mattie moved quickly over to his door. She stuck her head out into the stark and empty hallway, then closed the door quietly and whispered, "Custis, there's no lock!"

He eased out of bed, placed his hand over his abdominal bandages and grunted, "Help me push the bed over against the door."

"What?"

"You heard me. Come on, Mattie. Once we get started, it'll only take a minute or two."

"This is ridiculous," she said, but she helped him anyway.

Longarm was sore and still a bit light-headed, but the bed was on wheels and the job was easily accomplished. Pulling up his hospital nightshirt, he displayed his large and distended manhood.

"I'll bet you want it as bad as I do."

Mattie shucked off her dress and underclothing, and

15

when she climbed up on the bed, she leaned forward so that Longarm could kiss her large breasts whose nipples were already hard to his great amusement. "You look as ready as I am, Mattie."

"Let's stop the talk and get with the program," she ordered, grasping his throbbing tool in her hands and then scooting back so that she could bend over and take it into her mouth.

Longarm moaned and closed his eyes. "I'm feeling better already, honey!"

She laved his throbbing manhood with her tongue for a few minutes and took him in her mouth. Normally, this would have gone on for quite some time, but Mattie was nervous, so she climbed over him and eased down slowly.

"At least there's one part of me that isn't suffering," he said, grabbing her hips as she began to move up and down so that their union made soft, sucking sounds.

Mattie loved to make love and, after several minutes, she closed her eyes and began to get serious. Her bottom began to work vigorously over his rod and they were having a wonderful time when, suddenly, they heard a banging on the door.

"Open up in there!" a nurse shouted. "Why is this door blocked?"

"Oh no!" Mattie cried, starting to jump off the bed.

"Hold on," Longarm ordered. "We're going to finish what we started."

"But what will they think?"

"I couldn't care less," he said. "Come on, girl, let's get back to what matters!"

Mattie was nervous but Longarm was determined, and when the nurse outside couldn't budge the door open, they went at it again with even more intensity. And just when Mattie's eyes rolled upward and she bit the back of her hand to keep from crying out with intense pleasure, Longarm began bucking and pumping her full of his hot seed.

"Oh, Mattie!" he growled, hips still thrusting until his sack was empty, and he fell back feeling complete release. "That's what the doctor should have ordered."

Mattie was panting and tendrils of her blonde hair were plastered to her perspiring face. She half fell off of Longarm and rolled off the bed to land on the floor. At the same time, someone gave the door a tremendous shove, and it swung open to reveal Dr. Cutler and three red-faced nurses staring with shock and amazement.

"Oh, for crying out loud!" Cutler shouted. "I can't believe what I'm seeing here! Don't you people realize this is a *hospital*!"

Longarm grinned and took his time covering up his glistening and still proud and prominent member. "I just wanted to show you that I'm feeling a whole lot better than you think, Doc."

"This is outrageous!" Cutler shouted, his face red with embarrassment.

"Yes," the head nurse squawked. "It's unbelievable."

Longarm peeled the covers back to expose himself. "So does that mean that you'll discharge me?"

"You're finished here!" Cutler yelled. "I want you out of this hospital now."

Longarm glanced down at Mattie, still lying on the floor and looking as if she wanted to crawl under the bed. "Honey," he said, "would you hand me my clothes? They're in that dresser over by the window."

Mattie nodded sheepishly, then jumped up and hurried over to do as he'd asked. By the time she dropped his pants and shirt on the bed, the doctor and the stern-faced, domineering nurses had vanished.

"Well," Mattie said, "you did it."

"No," he corrected, "*we* did it."

Mattie shook her head. "I'd rather die than ever come back here to face them again."

17

"Ah," he said with a gesture of dismissal, "they probably see things like that every day."

"No they don't," Mattie said, taking a chair over by the window. "But at least we gave them something to talk about and long remember."

"That's right," Longarm said cheerfully. "Now will you help me with my boots and stockings?"

Longarm was discharged, and, with Mattie's help, he managed to get a carriage which took him straight over to the federal building on Colfax Avenue where the U.S. Marshal's Office was located. He had to walk up a flight of granite stairs leading from the street to the building's imposing entrance. That's when he realized he was still far sicker than he'd realized. Longarm began to cough so hard he had to sit down on the steps before he keeled over in a faint.

"Marshal Long! Are you all right! Do you need a doctor?" one of the older women who worked there asked, placing her hand on his shoulder.

Longarm shook his head. And when the coughing finally ended, he said, "Do me a favor, Mrs. Graham."

"Certainly!"

"Go up and ask Billy Vail to come down to see me. I feel like someone lit a fire in both my lungs."

"I'll be right back," she said. "Marshal Long, everyone is so proud of you for saving that boy. But you really shouldn't be . . ."

"Thanks, Mrs. Graham, but I'd sure appreciate it if you'd just go bring Mr. Vail."

"Of course."

Longarm perspired heavily although the day was cool and overcast. He was also shaking and felt awful. Perhaps he should have conserved his strength and sent word for Billy to come to the hospital. No matter. What was done, was done, and he wouldn't have traded anything for the shocked and outraged expressions on Dr. Cutler and the other bossy nurses' faces when they'd seen him and Mattie.

"Custis!" Billy said, hurrying down the stairs. "What the hell are you doing out here?"

"I was trying to make it to your office."

"You should be in the hospital."

"Give me a hand the rest of the way up the stairs."

"Dammit! I'm going to have a word or two with Dr. Cutler."

"Let it be," Longarm told his boss. "I sort of provoked the man, and he saw fit to give me an early discharge."

"What did you do? Oh, never mind. I don't even want to know. Easy now."

Billy was older and smaller and not in very good shape, thanks to having been riding a desk chair for too many years. Even so, with the man's help, Longarm was able to reach his office where Billy shut the door.

"This is insane!" Billy ranted. "Dr. Cutler told me that you were—under no circumstances—to exert yourself. Don't you remember him telling us how exertion could cause a rupture of the blood vessels in your lungs?"

"Billy," Longarm explained, using his handkerchief to wipe the cold sweat from his brow, "I just had to get out of that hospital. I was going crazy and ready to throttle some of those nurses with my bare hands. So I got Mattie McGuire to . . . well, never mind what I got her to do. The point is that I'm here and I'm ready to go to Arizona."

"I don't think you're up to the trip." Billy began to pace back and forth. "Custis, you look terrible. You've lost weight, and your skin is sallow. I think a long, difficult trip would finish you off."

"You're wrong," Longarm argued. "What I need is a change of scenery and some fresh air. Why, I never saw so many sick and dying people as I did in that hospital.

19

I think just being there is asking for a death sentence."

"You've always been headstrong and mule stubborn," Billy grumbled, "and I don't think you know what's best for your health."

"Maybe so and maybe not, but I want some travel money. Can you get it?"

"Right now?"

"Yes. The train heading south is leaving in about"— Longarm consulted his pocket watch—"in about two hours. I intend to be on it heading for Pueblo, Raton and Santa Fe. I can change over and be in Tucson in three days—four at the most."

Billy studied his best deputy marshal. "If it's any consolation, I did manage to get Mr. Pullman to agree that you should be on full pay while you convalesce. But he could only give you a couple of months."

"That's not very long," Longarm said, "but it ought to do. I expect to be back in shape by this fall. How will I get paid?"

"Wire me when you get to Tucson or wherever it is you'll be staying down in Arizona, and I'll wire back authorization for payments at whichever bank you choose."

"How about an advance on this month's full pay?"

"Sure," Billy said. "It's the least we can do for you after the heroism you displayed saving Donald Hamilton. Because of your efforts, Mr. Pullman has received a lot of good feedback and he certainly wants to congratulate you personally."

"If it was that important to the man, he would have come down to the hospital days ago."

"It wouldn't take long to stop by and it would be good for your career," Billy suggested.

Longarm didn't much care for their administrator. Horace H. Pullman was a bureaucrat who'd kissed enough federal fannies to get himself a job which he was not only unqualified to hold, but one in which he had no interest.

"Billy, tell the administrator that what I have in my lungs could be infectious, and that's why I thought it best to leave without first paying the man a visit."

"Is it?"

"What?

"Infectious?"

Longarm shook his head. "I don't think so. At any rate, go get me some money, and then help me off to my boarding house. I might need your assistance packing and getting to the train station."

"All right. Just sit still and keep the door closed. The fewer people that know you're in the building, the better."

"Sure." Longarm glanced over at the handsome humidor on Billy's desk. "While I'm cooling my heels, do you mind if I have a cigar?"

"Of course I mind! My gawd, man! A cigar might kill you."

Longarm just shrugged, but once Billy was gone he helped himself. The cigar tasted good, but he didn't dare inhale very deeply.

"All right then," Billy said, after giving Longarm a piece of his mind over his smoking. "Here's a hundred dollars, which ought to get you to Arizona . . . provided you don't die en route."

"I won't die."

"Pick a hot, sunny place down there, and do nothing but rest."

"Sure."

"No wild women."

"Of course not," Longarm said, keeping a straight face.

"And remember that you are on administrative sick leave, and, therefore, technically have no authority. That means you are just an *ordinary citizen* who has gone in search of rest and recuperation."

"Gotcha."

"All right then," Billy said. "Let's go and just hope that we can sneak back out of the building without notice."

"I'd like that."

Longarm stifled an urge to snatch up a few of Billy's excellent cigars for the train ride. Instead, he placed the envelope with money into his coat pocket and moved toward the door.

When they opened it, however, the hallway was filled with federal workers shouting and trying to pound Longarm on the back and extend their congratulations. And when they finally managed to get through the excited throng, who should be standing at the front entrance but Director Horace H. Pullman.

"Oh, damnation," Longarm muttered as the overstuffed, overpaid politician waddled forward to embrace Longarm.

"Marshal Long," Pullman began, "they told me that you were out of the hospital and in the building. Rather than trouble you to come to see me, I came right down here to see you."

It was all that Longarm could do not to gag. He forced a thin smile and said, "Thanks, sir."

"Well, thank *you!*"

Pullman stepped back and fell into his usual long-winded oration. Raising his arms to the crowd and grinning like a used-pot-and-pan salesman, he thundered, "Ladies and gentlemen, I know we all share pride in what Marshal Long has so nobly accomplished in Cherry Creek. And I'm here today not only to congratulate him for his extraordinary feat, but also to say that I appreciate the tremendous dedication that every last one of you show me in your work every single day here at the federal building. You know . . ."

Longarm didn't hear the rest of the speech because he thought he might vomit, which also wouldn't advance his career. So he turned on his heel and managed to get outside where the fresh air cleared his head.

"All right, Billy, keep me upright going down these stairs."

"Mr. Pullman is going to have a fit when he realizes you ducked out on his speech."

"He'll survive," Longarm replied. "Let's get me on the train headed south."

"Fine," Billy snapped back. "And guess who will take the heat for your bad manners?"

"You'll also survive," Longarm said as they started down the stairs. "So how are your wife and children?"

"They're all doing well."

"Good," Longarm said. "I'll send your son a souvenir from the Sonoran Desert."

When they reached the sidewalk, Billy said, "Just don't send a tarantula, scorpion or rattlesnake."

"Of course not," Longarm assured his boss and old friend with a smile, "I'd only send one of those scaly, poisonous critters to a backslapping blowhard like Mr. Pullman."

Billy burst out laughing.

Chapter 3

Longarm's trip south was uneventful until the westbound Southern Pacific reached Benson, Arizona, located about sixty miles east of Old Tucson. The weather was bright and balmy, and they had an hour layover, so Longarm decided it would be good for his health to get out and take a walk around town. He could stretch his legs, breathe deeply and try to shake off the lethargy that had come over him since he'd contracted pneumonia.

As he strolled about the old railroad town, he thought about Mattie and so many other women he had met and wondered if he'd ever get married and settle down to raise a family. Probably not. Longarm considered himself a restless man, and the idea of settling into a desk chair like Billy Vail left a bad taste in his mouth. Not that Billy and other married men with families had chosen the wrong path in life. No, it was just that marriage and family wasn't *his* life. And while many men were happily married, it was also true that plenty of others were miserable and felt trapped by their responsibilities.

"Afternoon, mister!"

Longarm turned to see a boy selling newspapers. "You interested in a paper, sir?"

"No, thanks."

The boy shrugged, trying to hide his disappointment. "Been a real slow day," he said, looking discouraged. "I can't seem to get hardly anyone to buy a paper. I guess all the railroad passengers are either broke or they just don't care about our town."

The boy was about twelve years old and poorly dressed. His feet were bare and he looked as if he had missed too many meals. Longarm was sympathetic. "How much is your paper?"

"Just a nickel."

"All right," Longarm said, handing the boy a coin. "I've got nothing to do but sit around until the train pulls out. I might as well read."

"Thanks, mister!" The boy's spirits seemed to have lifted. "Say, where you come from?"

"Denver."

"Are you going to California?"

"Nope. Just to Tucson."

"Too bad," the kid said. "I hear all the time from passengers about how the weather in California is the best. And I sure would like to see the Pacific Ocean. They say it's so big you can't begin to see across it. Do you reckon that's true, mister?"

"I expect it is." Longarm sat down in an empty chair in front of a barber shop. "What's your name?"

"Michael. Michael Page. My father was a lawman, but he got killed a couple of years ago. Someone shot him in the back of the head while he was makin' the rounds of the saloons one summer night."

"I'm sorry to hear that. What about your mother?"

"She works all the time trying to keep food on the table. I got three little brothers and sisters. We're doin' all right, and we don't ask for no charity."

"Well," Longarm said, trying to think of a way to give the kid a dollar without it looking like charity, "I sure am

26

curious about Benson, but I don't know who to ask about this town."

"Why, I know something about it! You can ask me darned near anything about Benson. You see, I have always lived here although I'm gettin' out as soon as I'm old enough, and I reckon it's my brother's turn to take care of Mother."

Longarm watched the procession of people moving up and down the street. He'd seen so many railroad and ranching towns like this one that he could guess what just about everyone did for a living. They were either in the cattle business, working for the Southern Pacific, a merchant or a clerk. Oh, or a mule skinner or a handyman. There really wasn't much else to do for a living in a town so small and poor.

"Did you know we have some rich men that live around these parts?" Michael asked.

"Nope."

"Well, we do. I'm going to be rich someday. I'll get to California and strike it rich in the goldfields. My pa used to talk all the time about striking it rich in the California goldfields, and I sure wished that he had, instead of getting himself shot to death."

"I expect that you do."

The boy pointed at a silver-haired man coming out of the town's only bank. He was dressed in a fine suit, expensive Stetson and wore a white starched collar. His beautifully stitched cowboy boots gave him away as a rancher, and Longarm guessed that the man was probably in his sixties. He walked erect and bore an unmistakable air of success and importance.

"See that old fella?" Michael asked.

"Yep."

"That's Mr. William Pendergast. He's a very rich man. He owns a big old guest ranch down south, somewheres near Tombstone. Lots of rich people get off the train here,

27

and he usually has a man pick them up and drive them down to his ranch to have fun and rest for a while. I don't know what it costs to stay there, but it must cost plenty. Mr. Pendergast is probably the richest man in the whole territory of Arizona."

"Well," Longarm said, "it's important to have enough money to enjoy life, but money isn't everything."

"It is to me," Michael said without a moment of hesitation. "Mister, if you got money, the world is your oyster."

Longarm had to smile. "Now who told you that?"

Michael shrugged. "I don't know. But someone did. Mr. Pendergast is real nice. He buys a paper from me every time he comes to town and you know what?"

"What?"

"He always tips me two bits." The boy smiled proudly. "That old gentleman is sure a nice fella. And you should see his only daughter, Miss Candice!"

When the kid's eyes widened, Longarm asked, "Is she a good-looker?"

"I'll say she is! She's also sweeter than any candy. Why, she even knows my name and always says hello when she comes to town. It don't mean a thing to me that she's been married once and that her husband died of pneumonia."

"I hear that can be bad."

"It is," the boy said. "Pneumonia will kill you quicker than tuberculosis any old day."

Longarm watched Pendergast move up the street greeting everyone he met in town. But then, something rang an alarm deep inside Longarm when he saw two rough workmen fall in step behind the old gentleman. They had emerged from between a couple of buildings and were keeping ten paces behind the rich man.

"There's a lot of men around here that sure would like

to marry Miss Pendergast, but her father sends them packing."

"Is that a fact?"

"Sure is! I think he worries that they want her for his money, but they're wrong, because she's so nice and also pretty."

"I see." Longarm was distracted. Ninety-nine out of a hundred people would not even have noticed how those two workmen carried themselves in a suspicious way, but Longarm had developed almost a sixth sense, and right now it was telling him that old Pendergast was being stalked.

"Michael, do you recognize those two men walking a little ways behind Mr. Pendergast?"

The boy squinted. "Nope."

Longarm decided he had no choice but to investigate. If he was wrong, and Mr. Pendergast wasn't in danger, then no one would even suspect that he'd been alarmed. Longarm folded his paper and laid it down in the chair saying, "I'll be back in a few minutes."

"Well, I got to run along and try to sell a few more newspapers," the boy said. "Nice talking to you."

"Same here."

Longarm was already heading up the street. He would follow the old man and the two tracking him until he made sure that he was mistaken about Pendergast being in danger. Had Longarm felt spry, he'd have used his long legs to quickly narrow the distance between himself and the men he followed. But he was feeling puny, so the best he could do was to close the gap slowly. He didn't know where the old man was heading, but wherever it was had to be near the outskirts of town.

A few minutes later, the wealthy old man entered a barn with the two roughnecks closing in on his heels. Just before entering the barn, the pair looked up and down the street, then apparently satisfied that no one was watching

29

their suspicious behavior, they disappeared inside.

They're up to no good, Longarm thought, wanting to break into a run but knowing that would likely cause him to fall prey to a fit of violent coughing. If that happened, he wouldn't be of any use to Pendergast or himself. Having no choice but to slow his pace, Longarm finally reached the barn, drawing his gun. He stepped inside the door just in time to see the two men knock Pendergast to the ground and begin viciously kicking him.

"Hey!" Longarm shouted. "United States Marshal. You're under arrest!"

The pair were bending over Pendergast, tearing through his pockets. And even though the light was poor, it appeared as if they had the old man's wallet and were trying to tear his gold pocket watch free.

"Don't move!" Longarm shouted.

The two men went for the guns on their hips. Longarm opened fire. He took his time, placing his shots with care, and, when he'd emptied four bullets into them, he knew that the thieves were dead.

Hurrying over to Pendergast, Longarm was gripped by a terrible cough so violent that he collapsed to his knees. He could see that the old man was hurt, but he couldn't do much to help him. At least the two thieves weren't going to trouble anyone ever again.

Longarm nearly passed out on the dusty floor of the livery barn. The cough felt as if it were tearing him asunder, and when he finally managed to get it stopped, he was left shaking as if he had the ague.

"Mister," Pendergast said, "you sound real bad. Is there anything I can do to help you?"

Longarm raised his head. The light was poor, but he could see that Pendergast had some nasty gashes on his face where he'd been struck and kicked by his two assailants. Longarm glanced over at them. One was still locked in his death throes.

"I'll go get help," Pendergast said, pushing to his feet and staggering toward the barn door.

Longarm heard the man shout, and then he was coughing again so hard he got dizzy and closed his eyes.

He awoke staring up at the blue sky, outstretched in front of the barn. Longarm asked for a drink of water, which revived him enough so that he could climb back to his feet.

"Stranger," Pendergast said, his face marred by one eye nearly swollen shut, "you saved my life."

"I should have come sooner, and then they wouldn't have had time to beat you up."

"I'll live," Pendergast assured him. "That pair would have beaten the life out of me if you hadn't arrived. But I sure am sorry about your terrible cough. For a while there, I thought we were going to lose you."

"I have pneumonia," Longarm explained. "I just need some rest and dry heat, which is why I'm on my way to Tucson."

Pendergast glanced toward the train depot. "I'm afraid that you missed your train. It pulled out about ten minutes ago."

Longarm saw that the train had, indeed, departed. "When is the next one coming through?"

"In a couple of days."

"That's not so bad," Longarm told him. "I can get a hotel room and wait."

"Boys," Pendergast said, straightening his tie and dusting off his fine suit of clothes, "fetch my carriage."

William Pendergast's carriage was a thing of beauty. Its brass hardware was polished to a shine, and the seats were of soft black leather. The carriage was pulled by four handsome and perfectly matched dapple gray geldings.

"Nice rig," Longarm said, as he was helped up into the carriage.

When Pendergast tried to climb into his carriage, he grunted with pain and clutched his side. "I think they cracked a rib or two."

"Mr. Pendergast," one of his men said, jumping down. "I'll give you a hand up!"

"Thanks."

The old rancher groaned as he was also helped into the carriage. He was pale, and Longarm could see that he was in a great deal of pain. "Maybe we should find a doctor. You're ribs might be broken."

"There's no doctor in Benson," Pendergast said. "Just an old quack who pulls teeth and sells snake-oil medicines. I'll be all right once I get back to the ranch and have a chance to rest."

"Are you sure?"

"Yeah," Pendergast answered, as one of his riders stepped up to drive them. "Just take it slow, Bob."

"Yes, sir!"

They drove back into town and stopped in front of a run-down building, the Apache Hotel. "This is all we have in town," Pendergast told Longarm, "and as you can see, it's a flea-infested hotel that looks even worse on the inside than it does on the outside."

Longarm remembered that his baggage was still on the train. That meant he'd have to buy a few toiletries to hold him over until he could reach Tucson and reclaim his belongings which, to be truthful, weren't all that valuable.

"Well," Longarm said, resigning himself to his sad circumstances, "I've stayed in a few hotels that look even worse."

"What's your name?" Pendergast asked.

"Custis Long."

"Mr. Long, I don't feel right about leaving you here."

Longarm forced a smile. "Don't give it a second thought. I'll sit out here on the porch and pass the time pleasantly enough. And the air feels good here, which will help clear my lungs and speed my recovery."

"Oh, there's little doubt about that," Pendergast assured him. "Some of my guests have made rapid and complete recoveries from their lung ailments."

"I'm glad to hear that."

Longarm started to climb out of the carriage, but the old man placed a hand on his sleeve. "Please do me the honor of repaying you for saving my life."

"That's not necessary."

"I'm not talking about money," Pendergast explained. "I want you to come out to my ranch and be my guest for as long as it takes for you to recover your health."

"Mr. Pendergast, the doctors back in Denver told me a recovery could take several months."

"Good! That means we'll have a lot of time to enjoy your company and get to know one another better."

"Sir, I appreciate your offer, but I couldn't . . ."

A powerful series of coughs rendered Longarm unable to finish what he'd been about to tell the old man. Gasping, wheezing and feeling truly miserable, he sagged in the carriage.

"That settles it, Mr. Long. You're coming out to our Tombstone Ranch until you're feeling better."

"But I don't even have any extra clothes. Everything I brought is on that train headed for Tucson."

"One of my men will handle that problem," Pendergast promised. "Now, not another word of argument. If you're up to the drive, we'll be at the ranch by sundown."

Longarm was in no condition to protest. He hadn't realized it, but they were surrounded by at least a half dozen of Pendergast's crew who looked very upset, probably at themselves, for not doing a better job of protecting their boss.

"You are very persuasive," Longarm told the rancher.

"Yes, I am. And I hope that you are not overly proud

and stubborn because you'd be passing up a nice place to rest and recover."

"Then I accept your offer."

"Splendid! And for now, just rest easy," Pendergast said. "I'm going to make sure that you make a full recovery and enjoy yourself in the meantime. Good food, good drink and good company are what I and my guests deserve!"

"Thank you very much."

"It's I that will forever be thankful to you," the older man said. "But I can tell you one thing."

"What's that?"

"I got in a couple of good blows before they knocked me to the barn floor and started kicking me. Yes sir, you probably couldn't see it, but I busted one of those sons of bitches in the eye and the other in the nose before they got me down and started kicking."

"Did you know them?"

"They were railroad trash. The kind that work when they are dead broke and then drink up all their money on payday. I should have been more alert that I was being followed."

"So should your crew," Longarm said.

Pendergast nodded. "It's hard to find people to take responsibility—especially when they are close to whiskey and loose town women."

"Yeah."

The carriage hit a pothole in the road, and the jolt brought a gasp of pain from the old man.

"Are you all right?" Longarm asked.

The old man had to wait a few seconds before he could speak. "I'll live, but I sure could use a couple shots of whiskey."

"Me, too."

"Bob, hold up the team!"

The driver reined in the horses. "Something wrong, sir?"

"Yes. Mr. Long and I are in serious need of my special liquid pain medicine."

"Whatever you say, Mr. Pendergast."

The driver set the brake and climbed down from his seat. Longarm saw him open a fine trunk in the back of the carriage, and then remove a bottle and two crystal glasses.

A few minutes later, they resumed their journey, but now Longarm and the old gentleman had full glasses of good whiskey cupped in their hands.

"Not bad," Longarm said, already feeling better.

Pendergast raised an eyebrow in question. "Why, Mr. Long, 'not bad' is quite the understatement. You see, this whiskey comes from Kentucky and costs ten dollars a bottle. In my opinion and the opinion of many of my guests, there is none better to be found."

"It's mighty fine," Longarm agreed, smacking his lips and feeling a warm glow fill his empty belly. "I sure do appreciate your hospitality."

"You haven't seen anything yet," Pendergast replied. "Once we get to the ranch, we're going to make sure that you have no reason to complain about anything. We cater to the rich, and they always expect the best."

"But I'm a long way from being rich. Why, you'd probably laugh if I told you how much money I make."

"I don't care if you're as poor as a beggar or as rich as a king. You are the reason why I'm still alive."

"Maybe that pair would have just been satisfied with taking your money and jewelry."

"I don't believe that," the man said. "They know I'm the kind that wouldn't have rested until they'd been brought to justice. For that reason, I'm pretty sure that they would have murdered me in order to keep from going to prison."

"Maybe so."

"But either way," Pendergast assured him. "From now on, you can have anything I have within my means to provide that will hasten your healthful recovery."

Longarm didn't quite know what to say, so he sipped his Kentucky whiskey and tried to breathe deeply of the warm and healthful Arizona air.

Maybe, he thought, *I've just gotten very, very lucky.*

Chapter 4

Longarm sat back in the carriage's soft leather seat and enjoyed the scenery. Mostly, it was high desert country with bunch grass and plenty of ocotillo, prickly pear and even a few of the giant, multiarmed saguaro cactus. It was a tough land, but he knew that this part of the Arizona Territory did not get nearly as dry or blazing hot as it did farther east over toward the old Yuma Crossing on the lower Colorado River.

"Mr. Pendergast, do you own any cattle?"

"We sure do," the old man answered, lighting up a cigar and offering one to Longarm, who was forced to decline because of his lungs. "We run about five thousand head down here on my Tombstone Ranch. All of these fellas you see riding along behind us are my regular cowboys, although they are expected to play nursemaid to my guests during the summer tourist season."

"Am I right to say that your primary income is from your winter guests?"

"Yes, it is. They can be difficult and extremely demanding, but they pay up front and in cash. You see, Custis, the cattle business can, and often does, go up and down. Before I bought the ranch, it had been owned by two other men who went bankrupt."

"Poor prices for beef?"

"That and the weather."

"The weather?"

"Some years we get a lot of rainfall and have plenty of good grass like you see coming up now. But other times, we hardly get a drop of rain, and this country almost dries up and blows away. When that happens, you can lose everything in a hurry. So I've tried to keep both the guest ranch and the cattle operation running together and not be completely dependent upon either for our livelihood."

"That makes sense."

"And I also run a few thousand head of sheep. I have Mexican herders, and they always bring a modest but reliable profit."

"So you believe in diversity?"

"I sure do. I try to spread my bets as far and wide as possible."

"Anything else bring you an income?"

"Yes, as a matter of fact. I raise and sell horses. Cow horses I keep, but I need plenty of good riding horses for my guests. And it doesn't hurt that quite a few of them fall in love with their mounts and insist on buying them."

"They ship Arizona horses all the way back East?"

"Sometimes, but often they retire the animal, claiming him only when they return each fall. In that case, I charge them a boarding and a handling fee."

"What's the 'handling fee'?"

"Well," Pendergast answered, "when you leave a horse alone in one of our fenced ranges for ten or eleven months of the year . . . he'll become half wild. Knowing that, I have to have a cowboy ride out and first catch the animal, then spend a week or so getting it reacquainted with the saddle and bridle. Some of the horses adjust well after their long vacation, but others can be very difficult."

"I see."

"Enough about me and Tombstone Ranch," Pendergast said. "What do you do for a living?"

"I'm a deputy United States marshal," Longarm quietly admitted.

Pendergast's eyes widened. "Well, you sure had me fooled. I figured you for either a professional gambler or perhaps a successful real estate speculator."

Longarm had to smile. "How'd you come up with that?"

"When you were unconscious, I had to take hold of your hand and I saw that they were smooth, without the kind of hard callouses that say a blacksmith, cowboy or any other man would have who did hard daily labor. Also, you dress well."

"Thanks, but I am a federal lawman," Longarm said, keeping his voice low. "Actually, Mr. Pendergast, I'd really prefer you not tell folks my profession."

"Why not?" the man asked, glancing up at their driver and now keeping his own voice down so they could not be overheard.

"When people learn what I do, some start to act funny."

"But why?"

"Because they might have done something illegal in their past and that causes them to become nervous and suspicious. First thing I know, they're either gone or they're thinking of ways to secretly do me in."

The rancher nodded with understanding. "That makes sense."

"It's been my experience," Longarm said.

"I'll keep your secret, but you're going to have a devil of a time hiding what you do from my daughter. She's curious and persistent. Candice will badger you until you tell her the truth."

"I don't mind telling you or your daughter. Can she also keep a secret?"

"I think so. Anyway, you'll find her entertaining. After her husband died, she went into a shell for a couple of years. Lost weight and didn't seem to care about anything. But she's come back now, and Candice is her old self."

"What about your wife and her mother?"

"Agnes died about five years ago. Heart trouble. Heart trouble seems to be the bane of our existence. That's what Candice's husband died of."

"The boy in town who sells papers said he died of pneumonia."

Pendergast shook his head. "James did have pneumonia. But he seemed to be on the mend when he suddenly took a bad turn for the worst. Next thing I know, he's dead. Not having a doctor around, we had to come up with some explanation, and when we took him into Tombstone to be buried, the undertaker said, from all appearances, it looked like poor James's heart just gave out under the stress of his lung ailments."

"I see. Do you have any other relatives?"

The rancher scowled. "I have a son who lives and works in Tombstone. He's a gunsmith, and he also works part-time as a deputy marshal. Vince and I just never could get along. He's not a bad young man, but he was always headstrong and difficult. I see him whenever I go into Tombstone, and we get along fine, so long as we don't talk politics, religion or about anything that matters to either one of us."

"No offense, sir, but it sounds like you both might be a bit stubborn."

Pendergast tossed his cigar stub and nodded. "That's probably more true than I care to admit. Anyway, Vince and Candice get along pretty well, and I suppose, when I'm gone, they'll both take over the ranch and do just fine. Both kids are hard workers."

"How old are they?"

"Candice is twenty-eight and Vince is thirty-two. He

40

has his eye on becoming the marshal of Tombstone, but his boss, Marshal Yates, shows no signs of retiring. Everyone likes Yates, and so do I. I think Vince is going to have to go find himself another town if he wants to advance."

"Did you ever talk to Vince about running a cattle and guest ranch?"

"Sure. But he really isn't interested. Now Candice is another matter. She actually enjoys ranching, and you should see how the guests love her. She gives them riding and shooting lessons. Tells them all about the famous Apache chiefs like Geronimo and Cochise that used to raise hell in this country. Everyone loves Candice."

"I'm sure that I'll like her as well."

"Just make sure that that's all you do with my daughter."

Longarm blinked with surprise and realized that Pendergast was quite serious. Given that his daughter was twenty-eight years old, the old man's reaction seemed overly protective, but Longarm said, "Sir, you've nothing to worry about."

"Candice is still young and pretty. Furthermore, because of the death of her husband, I fear she might be extremely vulnerable to the opposite sex and easily taken advantage of."

"I understand."

Pendergast relaxed. "Almost all of our guests are older, married folks, so Candice isn't presented with many temptations, and that's just the way I want it at the ranch."

"You've got a lot of cowboys," Longarm reminded the rancher.

"That's true," Pendergast said, "and they all know that if they want to keep their jobs, they stay far away from Candice."

"I'm a sick man," Longarm assured his host. "You've nothing to worry about in my case."

41

"Good! And by the way, since you saved my life and we're going to be friends, I'd appreciate it if you called me Will."

"I *will* do that."

The old man nodded and reached into his coat pocket for another cigar. "Candice says these things will kill me one day, but I'm too fond of smoking to even consider quitting. And besides, I've enjoyed cigars for nearly fifty years and they ain't done me in yet. I figure I'll die of something else first, and why deprive myself of whiskey and tobacco when life's pleasures are so few?"

"You seem to be doing all right in the pleasure department," Longarm observed. "This coach is the best one I've ever seen."

"It is nice," Pendergast readily agreed. "I had it specially made for me in St. Louis, and it cost three thousand dollars."

"That's a lot of money."

"Sure, but it was worth every penny. When my guests come into Benson on the train, often tired and irritable from the rigors of their long journey, I want them to go from first-class coach to first-class carriage. They pay a lot of money to come down here, and they expect the best."

"That makes sense."

Pendergast lit his cigar and tossed the match aside. "Custis, have you always been a lawman?"

"Nope. I've done plenty of things, but I like what I do now, and most people seem to think I'm good at it."

"I'll bet you are! Being tall and broad shouldered, you even look like you ought to be a lawman."

"More than a gambler or real estate speculator?"

Pendergast chuckled until his ribs acted up, and he doubled over in pain.

"Take it easy," Longarm urged. "Those ribs will bear

looking after when we get to your ranch. How much farther?"

"We're on it now, but we won't get to the ranch house for another hour."

"Big ranch."

"Down in this country, they have to be big," the older man explained as he reached for the whiskey and a refill of his glass. Longarm figured he might as well have another drink as well. He breathed in deeply of the warm desert air and his lungs already felt much improved.

The buildings were arranged in a semicircle around a manicured lawn, and all were freshly painted white. Longarm's first impression was how dramatically they stood out in contrast to the blue sky, the distant brown hills and even more distant purple mountains. Pendergast's ranch house had a big veranda that reminded him of a southern mansion. It was a two-story building, and someone had planted climbing red roses which now adorned a wall of trellises and offered a brilliant splash of color to the tranquil and elegant setting. Longarm had to admit that the place was right out of a picture book, but it looked as if it belonged someplace other than in this hard Arizona landscape.

"What do you think?" Pendergast asked, obviously proud of his home.

"It's impressive, and I'll bet has a lot of rooms."

"Twenty-two," the rancher boasted. "The main house has seven guest bedrooms, but of course, the paying guests stay in the surrounding cottages. However, they all come to eat in the big house with Candice and me. We try to treat them like family without getting too involved in their lives. The first of our guests ought to be arriving in about a week. I want to be up and moving around good when they get here."

"Does your daughter do all the cooking?"

"Not a chance. I employ a couple of women who are excellent cooks and housekeepers, and I pay them both top dollar. Candice is supposed to oversee our kitchen staff and be responsible for the menus and making sure that everyone is happy with their meals. But instead, she's always outdoors either working in the flower gardens or with the horses and livestock. She's a ranch girl. Took to it right away, and I doubt she'll ever change. That's her coming out on the porch right now."

Longarm saw a beautiful young woman of average height with long, light brown hair emerge. She waved, and when Pendergast had difficulty lifting his arm to return the greeting, Candice flew down the stairs and out to meet their carriage.

"Father!" she cried, "Your eye is swollen shut and your face is bruised. What happened?"

"Oh," he said, trying to make light of his discomfort, "I had a little trouble in Benson and hurt my ribs."

"Your ribs? What about that black and swollen eye?" Candice turned to the carriage driver. "Bob, what's wrong with Father?"

"Miss Candice, he got hurt when two men tried to rob him in the Benson livery barn. Me and the boys all feel terrible about it, and that's the truth."

The young woman's eyes sparked with anger. "Regrets mean nothing when it comes to taking care of my father. Where were you and the others during the attack?"

Bob lowered his eyes and muttered something that sounded like an apology.

"Well! Where were *all* of you?" Candice demanded, eyes raking Bob and the collection of mounted cowboys that had followed along behind them.

"Now, now," Pendergast said, trying to smooth over the situation. "Candy, you know that these boys work hard out here and that I like them to have their little pleasures when they get to town."

"Father, I don't give a good gawdamn about their 'little pleasures'! They're supposed to watch out for *you*. That's part of what they get paid to do!"

The old man raised his hand to indicate he wished his daughter to hold her harsh judgment in silence. "Throwing blame around isn't going to do any good. Let's just simmer down, and let me introduce the man who did happen to come along just in the nick of time and kill the pair of thugs that attacked me."

Candice's eyes turned to Longarm, and she seemed to take him all in with a glance. "Mister, I am grateful for what you did and that goes for killing the men who tried to hurt my father."

"Ma'am, we need to get your father into the house and examine his ribs."

Candice nodded with understanding and said, "I'll run back into the house, and we'll lay him down on the cowhide couch. Do we need to send off to Tucson for a doctor?"

"We'll know soon enough," Longarm told her.

They brought Will Pendergast in and laid him down on the living room couch; then, Longarm watched as Candice unbuttoned her father's shirt and drew back in shock at the sight of his purplish ribs and chest.

"What did they do to him?" she cried, twisting around to glare at Bob and several of the other cowboys.

"Easy," the rancher groaned. "There's no point in getting all upset. Those that did this to me have paid dearly for their mistake, thanks to our new friend, Custis Long."

"But all your ribs must be broken," Candice said, her voice sick with worry.

Longarm knelt down beside the man and gently placed his fingers on the old man's rib cage. "This is going to hurt a little, but it'll tell me if you need to see a doctor."

"Hell, I don't want to see a doctor! Nearest real doctor is fifty miles away."

Longarm had broken and cracked many ribs in his life-time, and, now, as he gently probed and prodded, he made his diagnosis. "They're not broken," he said. "Just cracked and mostly bruised."

Pendergast grinned. "Did you hear that, Candy? I'm going to be a new man tomorrow. Just you wait and see."

"He's no doctor."

"That's true," Longarm admitted, "but I've had my share of injuries, and I can tell you that a good doctor would have us bind up those ribs and keep them bound up for the next week or ten days. After that, your father will be able to get around and be on the mend."

She looked up at him closely, and he could tell she wanted to believe his diagnosis. "Custis, are you abso-lutely sure? What if there is some internal damage to an organ that we don't know about?"

"That can happen, but it's rare."

"All right then," Candice said. "I'll go find some band-aging and we'll do it your way."

When she returned, she was accompanied by a woman about her own age who had long black hair drawn back sharply from her face and tied in a bun. Her eyes were large and hooded, and her complexion left little doubt that she had at least some Indian or Mexican blood flowing in her veins.

Candice introduced the young woman. "Donita, this is . . ."

"Custis Long," he said. "Pleasure to meet you."

Donita gave him the briefest of smiles, and then helped Candice bind up the old man's ribs.

"Not too tight," Longarm warned.

"You think you can do it better?" Candice asked point blank.

"No, but . . ."

"Then please do not offer your opinion."

Longarm was slightly taken aback by Candice's sharp

tone, and so was her father, because he said, "Honey, that's no way to talk to the man that saved my life."

"I'm sorry," Candice said, looking as if she meant it. "I'm just . . . just upset."

"You have every right to be," Longarm told her. "But everything is going to turn out fine."

"I sure hope so. People die suddenly, you know."

Longarm thought that was an odd thing for the rancher's daughter to say, until he reminded himself that her husband had died suddenly and unexpectedly.

"Donita," Pendergast grunted. "Show our guest upstairs to one of the west wing bedrooms. He's going to be staying with us until he recovers from a bout of pneumonia."

"He could room in one of the guest cottages," Candice said.

"Nope. He saved my life, and he's part of the family now . . . as long as he behaves like a gentleman."

Pendergast's eyes flicked from Longarm to his daughter, and his meaning could not have been clearer.

"You rest easy," Longarm said, as he started to follow the housekeeper. "I'll be back down in awhile to see how you're doing."

"Don't bother," Pendergast called out across the huge living room with its floor-to-ceiling stone fireplace. "You need to rest and recover as much as I do."

Longarm figured that was true. He was bone tired, but not so much that he couldn't admire Donita's pretty ankles as she mounted the stairways with him following in her wake.

"This way," she said when they reached the top of the landing. "Will you be staying long, Mr. Long?"

"I hope so."

Donita was graceful, and as she led him down a hallway with plush carpeting and original artwork, Longarm couldn't help but imagine what she would be like in bed.

But then he chided himself, because he'd promised the

old rancher that he would behave himself at Tombstone Ranch. And besides, he needed to rest and recuperate, not get involved with this pretty housekeeper or the rancher's daughter.

At least, that's what he reminded himself as Donita showed him to a beautifully appointed bedroom with a massive bed, chest of drawers and an unusual chair fashioned out of the horns of an elk, bound and padded with soft buckskin.

Chapter 5

That night, Longarm was awakened by shouts from the living room. He quickly dressed and went to see the cause of all the commotion.

"It's Father!" Candice cried, kneeling beside the old rancher who was still resting on the couch. "He's in terrible pain."

Longarm glanced at Donita, and then he went over to kneel beside Pendergast. Candice was right. Her father was in pain and his condition had seriously deteriorated since their arrival.

"Where does it hurt?" Longarm asked.

"I feel like I'm on fire," Pendergast answered, his voice weak and breathless. "I must have a fever."

Longarm placed his hand on the man's forehead. He twisted around and said, "Get some cold water, and we'll use compresses to try and drop his temperature. Hurry!"

Both women hurried off to the kitchen. "Will, describe the pain."

"It's like a toothache, only it's in my belly," the man replied. "Every little while I feel a sharp, stabbing pain in my guts, like they're exploding."

Longarm wasn't a doctor, but he could see that the man

was in agony, and that did not bode well for recovery.

"What's the matter with me?"

"I don't know. I'm not sure that a doctor would know. Maybe you've suffered a ruptured appendix or spleen. Or perhaps there's a tear in your liver because of the force of the blows. I can't say for sure. All I know is that we'd better get you to a doctor right now."

"No!" Pendergast gripped his arm. "Custis, I can't take the jolts of fast travel. I can barely stand the pain just lying here on this couch."

"Well, we've got to do something." Longarm glanced up at the women who came rushing back with cold compresses. "Candice," he said, "you need to send for a doctor."

"But it's sixty-five miles to Tucson!"

"It's all we can do," Longarm said. "If you send a rider with a couple of relay horses, he can be there before daybreak and return with a doctor by this time tomorrow night."

"But . . ."

"Do it!"

Candice nodded and ran out the front door. Longarm knew she was going to go to the bunkhouse and awaken the cowboys and that the best and lightest rider would be sent off within fifteen minutes. The trouble was, from the looks of the rancher, it was going to be a long, desperate ride for nothing.

"Custis," Pendergast said. "I want to talk to you in private."

"Me?"

"Yes. Listen to me closely. I don't trust my son with this ranch. He's . . . he's not an honest man. If I should die, I want you to make sure that Candy isn't taken advantage of by Vince."

"But, sir, I . . ."

Pendergast's fingernails bit into Longarm's wrist.

"Please," he begged. "I got no one else to ask. If you want me to sign an agreement for cash in return for your services, I'll do that, but . . ."

Pendergast suddenly cried out, and his entire body went rigid. His mouth opened wide in a silent scream and his eyeballs seemed to bulge from their sockets. Longarm couldn't help it . . . he momentarily recoiled in horror.

"Mr. Pendergast!" Donita cried. "Candice, come quick!"

"Father!" Candice shouted, racing back to his side and hugging him tightly.

Longarm retreated and watched as the old man's feet and hands began to shake. Then, he saw Pendergast's body convulse, and he heard an ominous death rattle as the old rancher struggled in vain to get air.

"Father!"

Pendergast reached up and his fingers got tangled in his daughter's long blonde hair a moment before they fell away.

"No!" Candice screamed.

Longarm looked at Donita and saw tears in the housekeeper's eyes. He turned away and walked out on the veranda. The cowboys were racing across the yard getting horses ready to relay the sixty miles to Tucson. Longarm stepped down from the veranda and took a deep breath. Someone had to tell them that there was no longer any need to go for a doctor.

William Pendergast was dead.

The funeral was well attended. Vince Pendergast was asked to say a few words in memory of his father, but he was too choked up to say anything. That was the way of it with sons and fathers sometimes. They might fight their whole lives, but when one or the other died, they were devastated. Vince was a tall, good-looking man, but his hair was long and greasy, and he had an unkempt and slightly dissipated air about him that brought back Pendergast's dying warning that his son was not to be totally trusted.

Candice was devastated. In the two days since the death of her father, she seemed to have aged ten years. Her eyes were swollen and bloodshot, and her movements were still. It seemed impossible that Longarm had once thought of her as beautiful. And yet she was, and, if she could manage to recover from the sudden and tragic losses of both her husband and her father, she would probably regain her looks and zest for life.

However, there were no guarantees. Longarm had seen a lot of death and grief both in the war and in his profession. And sometimes, people who suffered great personal losses never did recover their vitality and spirit.

Three days after the funeral, Candice told him that she had decided, because of her father's death, to wire the first of their visitors that the Tombstone Ranch would no longer be accepting its usual winter guests.

"Are you sure that's a good idea?" Longarm asked. "Your father told me that the guests are a large part of this ranch's income. He was proud of the fact that you're diversified, and he said that the easterners who come here really love their visits and the way you teach them the local Apache lore as well as how to ride and shoot."

"I just don't think that I could do it this winter," Candice confessed. "I can't laugh and pretend to be having a good time when I ache inside for the loss of my father. After my mother died, Father was my strength. And, after my husband died, he was again my strength. But now . . . even he is gone."

"What about your brother, Vince?"

Candice shook her head. "He's insisting that we make no changes. Vince is adamant that we bring the paying guests back and go on as if nothing happened. Only something *has* happened!"

They were sitting on the same cowhide-covered couch that William Pendergast had died upon. "Look," Longarm said, searching for the right words to convey his troubled thoughts, "I didn't know your father well, and I can't say that I understand why he died. He must have had some internal injuries that none of us could detect."

"It's not your fault. Even if there had been a doctor in attendance, I'm convinced that it wouldn't have saved Father's life."

"I agree. Candice, before I came here I was impaled by a tree limb while trying to save a drowning boy."

Her eyes widened. "How terrible!"

"It was a serious wound. The Denver doctor worried that I would get peritonitis—an infection of the abdominal cavity—and die. That's probably what happened to your father. When those men kicked him in the side so viciously, they must have ruptured an organ, and its spilled contents poisoned his system."

Candice's eyes filled with tears. "I guess that would explain why he died so unexpectedly."

"Yes, it would. Your father loved this ranch and was very proud of its success. He specifically mentioned how the previous owners had gone bankrupt and vowed that would never happen to him. Candice, your father would have wanted you to do whatever it takes to keep Tombstone Ranch. But, if you give up the best part of its income, the day might very well come when you lose it just like the previous owners."

"So you agree with Vince that I should do the best I can and go on as if nothing happened?"

"That is going to be impossible, but I do think you ought to try and get through this winter tourist season."

"Can you stay and help?"

He smiled. "I'm battling my own illness. Remember?"

"Of course. It was shameless of me to ask."

"That's all right. I'm feeling better already. It's probably snowing in Denver, and this warm southwest climate is making me feel almost chipper."

"I'm so glad you came and that you got to know Father before he died."

"So am I. Will Vince stay in Tombstone or will he move out here to help you run the ranch?"

"I don't know," she said. "He likes the town life. Vince has a lot of friends in Tombstone, and he enjoys the saloons and dance halls too much to isolate himself out here. But I really do need his help."

"Do you want me to talk to him?"

"Would you?"

"Sure," Longarm said. "Maybe you could get Bob or one of the boys to hitch up a small buggy, and I'll drive into town. How far is it?"

"Less than ten miles. Donita is going into Tombstone to buy groceries. You could go along with her tomorrow morning."

"That would be fine."

"Listen," Candice said, "about my brother. He can be rude and obnoxious. If he thinks you're trying to get him to do one thing, he'll almost always do the other."

"So you're telling me not to pressure him."

"That's right. He told me at the funeral that, unless I want to make him the one in charge of everything, he wouldn't lift a finger to help. Can you imagine?"

"Does he know a lot about running a ranch?"

"No," Candice said.

"Then let's just see how it goes," Longarm said. "I'm not in the habit of begging anyone to do something."

"Thank you for saving my father. In just the little time that you were together, I could see that he really liked you."

"And I liked him. Candice, just try and be strong, and you'll get through this. And perhaps before long you'll meet another man and fall in love. Then you'll have a partner and be happy once more."

She looked into his eyes. "Yes," she said. "One can always hope that love is just around the corner. But the truth is, everyone I've ever loved . . . I've lost. I feel, well, almost like a pariah. That I'm cursed."

"That's not true."

"I sure hope not. I'm almost afraid to love again."

Longarm understood, and when Candice walked away, he wondered what else he could have said or done to make the poor woman feel better.

Chapter 6

Longarm slept well that night and arose at sunrise. He dressed, shaved, slipped on his gunbelt and placed his badge in his coat pocket. Grabbing his hat and running his fingers through his hair, he then went into the kitchen looking for a cup of coffee. Donita was already fixing breakfast at the big stove, and when she looked up and saw Longarm, she smiled. "Are you hungry, Custis?"

"I could eat."

"Then sit down, and I'll bring you coffee and breakfast."

"Thanks."

The coffee was steaming hot, black and strong, just the way he preferred. And while Donita rustled up some eggs, bacon and pancakes, Longarm had a chance to wake up and to admire both her looks and her efficiency.

"There you go," she said, setting the plate of hot food down in front of him. "I hope you're hungry."

"I am," he said, looking at the huge stack of pancakes, the half dozen thick slabs of bacon and just as many eggs. "But I don't know if I can eat all this."

"You are too thin. You need to eat more."

Donita sat down at the table across from him. The hour

was still very early and they were apparently the only ones awake in the ranch house. She sipped at her own coffee and stared out the window as the sun rose in the east. It gave Longarm the chance to study her strong face with its high cheekbones. Donita had full lips, thick dark eyebrows and a dusky, flawless complexion. But she suddenly turned her head and caught him studying her.

"Do you stare at all women?"

"Only the beautiful ones."

Donita blushed and said nothing, but instead drank more coffee, then got up and fixed herself a breakfast plate. When she returned to the table, she began to eat.

"Will we be leaving pretty soon?"

She looked up. "Oh, yes. Within the hour. Soon, man will bring us a buckboard up to the house, and then we will go to Tombstone."

"I'm looking forward it," Longarm told her. "I'm getting restless hanging around the house. I've read several of Mr. Pendergast's books that I borrowed from his library, but I'm not one to sit around in the daytime at my ease."

"Me, neither," she said.

"Been working here long?"

"Yes. I worked for the family that lived here before this one. They were not as nice, and I was very young. Mr. Pendergast was a good man, and I miss him very much."

"I'm sure that his daughter counts heavily on your friendship and service," Longarm told the young woman.

"Miss Candy is . . . is fine."

Longarm thought he detected some reservations in that remark and that surprised him. But then again, when one person worked for another, it was always difficult, if not impossible, for them to be close personal friends. The only reason that he and Billy Vail were close was because Longarm was gone so often doing investigative work.

"I expect that you will be staying here," Longarm said, just trying to make conversation.

She looked up at him with those large and luminous dark eyes that he found so interesting. And then she said absolutely nothing.

Longarm decided that it might be a good idea to drop the personal questions. It seemed clear that, while on the surface the two young women of the house were friendly, there was no great love between Donita and Candice.

"What do you do when you are not recovering from the lung illness?" she asked.

Longarm really didn't want her or the others to know of his true profession for the reasons that he'd given to Pendergast before the man had died.

"I keep busy," he said, aware of how vague that sounded. "And I like to travel."

She suddenly looked at him with real interest. "Have you been to many far away and exciting places?"

"Not so far away or exciting. I've never been to other countries . . . except for Mexico. But I have traveled through much of the West."

She studied her coffee. "I would like to see more of this country and even the whole world. First, though, I would like to see the Grand Canyon and the Pacific Ocean."

"Well, I'm sure that you will some day."

"Maybe," Donita told him. "You see, I am poor and . . . unless that changes for some reason . . ."

She left the statement hanging and looked directly into his eyes. Longarm had the feeling that she was measuring him very closely.

They ate the rest of their breakfast in silence, and when Longarm was finished, Donita scooped up their dishes and utensils and washed them in a sink with hot water she had heated on the stove. When she was done with her kitchen work, she disappeared upstairs.

There was a knock on the front door, and Longarm went to answer it. Bob was standing on the veranda with his hat in his hand. "I understand that you're goin' into Tombstone with Donita."

"That's right."

"Well," the middle-aged cowboy said, "normally I take her in because it's not good to have a woman out on the road alone. The Apache are mostly peaceable now, them that haven't been killed or shipped off somewheres. But there are bad whites, and Mr. Pendergast never would allow a woman of his employ to be out on the road without a man and a gun."

"I understand."

"So," Bob said, "since I can see you're packin' a six-gun, I reckon I don't need to go to Tombstone, and I can do my ordinary work today."

"That's right," Longarm told the slow-talking cowboy.

"Good enough." Bob started to turn away, then stopped and said, "You gonna stay on here at Tombstone Ranch for quite some time, are you?"

"I don't know for sure exactly how long it will take to get healthy. Why do you ask?"

The cowboy shifted his boots nervously. "It's just that it doesn't look right for a single man to be living alone in the same house with Miss Candice. No disrespect, but it just don't, and it'll cause a lot of the guests to talk."

"I hadn't even thought of it, but you're probably right," Longarm said. "Is there any room for me to put up in the bunkhouse?"

Bob grinned. "Well, sir, it's pretty rough and mean in the bunkhouse, but I reckon there's a vacant guest cottage that you could use. It'll be empty until just before Christmas when a family from Ohio is due to arrive."

"Then that's where I'll sleep."

Bob looked relieved. "Glad you can understand the situation. As we both know, Miss Candice is a real fine

60

woman, and we have to think of her reputation."

"That's right."

"Well," the cowboy said, "I better get about my regular business. There's strays that need catchin' and brandin', and the buckboard is all ready for you and Donita. Just be careful in Tombstone. There's some real rough fellas hang out there. The Earp boys are long gone, and Sheriff Behan never was worth beans."

"I understand that Vince is a deputy marshal."

Bob looked away for a moment, then turned back and said, "Just between us and the fence post . . . Vince ain't worth the powder it would take to blow off his nose even if he is fast with a gun. He pins on a badge and works for Marshal Yates, but they don't do much except roll drunks and collect a few dollars from the town. Tom Yates is worthless, and Vince Pendergast is happy just following his lead."

"That's too bad."

"Yep. What I'm trying to tell you is that Tombstone started out wild soon after gold and silver was first discovered there by Ed Schieffelin about ten years ago and it's gone downhill ever since. Fires wiped the town out in the summers of eighty-one and eighty-two, but everyone was makin' so much money they rebuilt the town with brick and stone so it couldn't burn again. But it's still rough and dangerous."

"I'll watch out over Donita."

"I'd appreciate that," Bob said. "She's a handsome woman, but as long as she stays on the south side of Allen Street, she ought to be just fine."

"The south side?"

"Yes, sir. The north side is the bad side. That's where you'll see all the saloons, dance halls and whorehouses. If a woman walks on the north side of Allen Street, she's fair game and expected to be ready, willin' and able. If you know what I mean."

"I know what you mean," Longarm said. "What's on the good side of Allen street?"

"Oh, the usual you'll find in any town. Barber shop. Bank. Newspaper office. Cafes. Respectable businesses. Tombstone even has a couple of churches. The biggest is St. Paul's Episcopal Church at the corner of Safford and Third Streets."

"But no doctors?" Longarm asked.

"The last two were bullet riddled like cheese when their patients died of gunshot wounds. Since then, I guess the word got out that Tombstone is good business for the undertakers, but hell to pay on doctors."

Donita appeared with a hat and a pretty green silk scarf tied around her neck. "Are we ready, Bob?"

"Yep. You be careful in town."

"I am always careful in Tombstone," she said. "But I can take care of myself."

"There's already a lot of folks buried in that new cemetery that probably thought the same."

Donita gave the man a tolerant smile and stepped down from the veranda. "You worry too much."

Longarm offered his arm to Donita, and she climbed up onto the seat. He followed and took the reins, recognizing the two horses as the ones who had been matched with another pair to pull Pendergast's elegant carriage when it brought him down from Benson.

Longarm released the brake, and the horses moved smartly forward. "Point me in the right direction," he said.

"That way," Donita told him, gesturing toward the southeast. "Just follow the road, and it will lead us to town."

Longarm breathed deeply of the clean, high desert air. The sun was out, and although it would be a bright, sunny day, it would not be particularly hot, which was just fine. No, the day would be pleasant and a little balmy and just perfect to take a nice outing with a lovely young woman.

He reminded himself that, if there was a telegraph office, he needed to check in with Billy Vail. Thinking of his boss, he could almost imagine a blizzard raging in Denver and poor Billy Vail and the others who worked in the federal building slipping and sliding on the ice and snow as they made their freezing journey up Colfax.

Boy, he thought, *I'm sure glad I'm in warm and sunny Arizona.*

Tombstone was a hard-looking town surrounded by rocks, cactus and sun-blasted hills. It always amazed Longarm to see the god-awful places where prospectors had ventured in search of a bonanza. He'd seen the barren, inhospitable country around the famous Comstock Lode in Nevada, but the landscape where Tombstone was located was every bit as harsh and unforgiving. Lying a few miles east of the San Pedro River and near the dangerous Dragoon Mountains, its major gold- and silver-bearing lodes were the Grand Central, Contention and Lucky Cuss. Donita explained that the entire town was built over a honeycomb of deep and shallow tunnels and stopes. Occasionally, one would collapse; the last time that had occurred, a team of mules and a freight wagon had been swallowed up by the earth.

"They call it 'The Town Too Tough to Die'," Donita said as they drove up Allen Street, passing Fremont and Toughnut Streets, as well as the Tombstone Epitaph newspaper office before pulling up in front of Baker's Mercantile.

"It'll die when the ore runs out. Always happens that way," Longarm replied.

"I suppose." Donita climbed down to the street. Looking up at him, she said, "It will take me about two hours to do my shopping."

Longarm studied the town. There were a lot of idle men standing around drinking and eyeballing passersby. He and the beautiful Donita had gotten more than their share of penetrating stares. "Do you need some help?"

"No, thanks."

"I wouldn't mind."

"Thank you," she said, "but I will be just fine. Look around and enjoy yourself. Have a beer or two."

"I just might do that," he decided. "Where can I find the telegraph office?"

"Up past the county courthouse and the Big Cage Theater," she said. "You can't miss it."

"Thanks." He checked his pocket watch. "I'll see you back here in about two hours?"

"Yes, but I could take a little longer."

"I've got nothing to do, so don't hurry."

After giving Longarm a bright smile, Donita went inside the mercantile. With nothing to do other than to send off a telegram to Billy, Longarm took care of the horses, then strolled down the boardwalk, peeking in the shops and taking his leisure. He stopped in front of Schieffelin Hall, named in honor of the town's discoverer and read a little sign that told him the building was the world's tallest adobe and the cultural and theatrical center of Tombstone. There were cheap flyers posted all over the front double doors advertising the upcoming winter performances.

After finding the telegraph office, Longarm sent his message to Billy briefly explaining why he had not gone on to Tucson as planned. He instructed the telegraph operator as to where he was staying and said, "I'll be coming in every week or ten days to check to see if I have any messages."

"Yes, sir. Are you . . . a federal marshal?"

There was no point of denying it, since he'd had no choice but to send his message to the federal building. "I have been given a sickness leave of absence because of pneumonia. And I'd appreciate it if you didn't tell anyone that I am a lawman. I'm here to rest and relax."

"You can count on me," the man promised. "And I want to say that those of us who knew and admired Mr. Pendergast were deeply saddened by his sudden death. It was quite a shock even though he was getting up in years."

"Yes, he did seem to be in excellent health," Longarm said. "But when the heart goes, it usually takes a person by complete surprise. I understand that is exactly what also happened to Miss Pendergast's late husband."

"Yep," the man agreed. "Although Jim was never in especially good health, and he did have his excesses."

"Oh?"

The telegraph operator, a small, nervous-looking man in his forties with thick spectacles balanced on a crooked and hooked nose, lowered his voice even though they were alone. "Jim drank pretty hard, and he also liked to go to the Chinese opium dens."

"Is that a fact?"

"It is," the operator said, bobbing his head up and down. "No one who ever knew the family could figure out why Miss Candy married that man other than the fact that he was from a wealthy Boston family and was said to have inherited quite a large estate."

Longarm hid his surprise. "Well, he's gone, and so is Mr. Pendergast, which all goes to prove that we can't take life for granted and that we'd better enjoy ourselves while we can."

"Exactly so!" the telegraph operator agreed. "And I hope you have a full and speedy recovery."

"Thanks."

Longarm went back down Allen Street, but he crossed the street to the north side wanting a couple of beers. After strolling along for a block or two, he entered the Crystal Palace Saloon because it looked to be the town's biggest and best drinking and gambling establishment.

The Crystal Palace was impressive, with its great hanging crystal chandeliers and long polished bar. The place was fairly quiet with only about a dozen customers, but that was because the hour was still early. Longarm suspected that this saloon would soon be packed with roisterous miners, cowboys, freighters and merchants.

He bought a beer and a cigar, then moseyed over to a quiet corner table where he placed his back to the wall, as was his habit, and propped his feet up on the seat of an empty chair. The saloon was dark and cool, and the familiar barroom banter and smells were a welcome change from the more formal atmosphere at the Tombstone Ranch.

Longarm had to strain his eyes to read his fine Ingersoll railroad pocket watch and saw that he still had over an hour to wait before meeting Donita back at the mercantile. That meant that he could enjoy at least one more beer and cigar.

About fifteen minutes later, Deputy Marshal Vince Pendergast marched into the saloon, and the congenial mood evaporated like mist in the sun. This was not entirely surprising to Longarm, for he had experienced the same effect when he had often entered a saloon in search of a fugitive. Longarm could feel the sudden tension as Vince leaned over the bar and whispered something to the bartender, who motioned him toward a back room.

Longarm's interest was piqued, but he did not think much about Vince, and about ten minutes passed before the deputy marshal appeared again. Suddenly, Vince drew his six-gun, pivoted on one heel and fired in one of the fastest, smoothest draws Longarm had ever witnessed.

At the end of the bar, a tall, thick-chested man cried out as he tried to drag up his own gun. Vince fired two more times, each of his bullets striking the man in the chest and knocking him back a step until he crashed over a spittoon. There wasn't any doubt that the man was dead before he landed on his backside in the sawdust.

Vince then walked over to the dead man and brazenly emptied his pockets of a thick roll of cash, the rings from his fingers and even his gold pocket watch. When he straightened, Vince said to no one in particular, "This man's name was Earl Jessup, and he was wanted in Tucson for murder. I gave him what he deserved. Anyone have any problem with that?"

No one, including Longarm, said a word. Vince either didn't recognize him or didn't care because he turned his back on the shocked patrons of the Crystal Palace Saloon and left without another word.

Longarm went over to join the other saloon patrons as they stood in an uneasy semicircle around Jessup. "Anyone ever see this fella before?" the bartender asked.

"I knew Earl Jessup," a miner whispered, shaking his head. "He owned a livery, and he wasn't from Tucson. I met him over at Bisbee mining camp, and he seemed like a fine, upstanding fella. I believe he even had a wife."

"Dammit," another said, his voice filled with anger. "I thought the law was supposed to arrest a man and see that he got a fair trial. What happened here was nothing but an execution!"

"You're right," Longarm said, because the man had echoed his own sentiments. He knelt beside Jessup and found a two-shot derringer and Bowie knife.

"How's his family even gonna know he was gunned down by Marshal Pendergast?" someone asked.

"I'll send a message to the telegraph office in Bisbee," Longarm decided aloud. "Someone will notify his wife, and she'll have to come here and claim his body. Until then, I think we ought to take up a collection for the man's family."

Longarm removed his hat and passed it around. The patrons were generous, and he collected at least fifty dollars.

The bartender said, "Who are you, mister?"

"My name is Custis Long."

"Well," the bartender said, voicing a reasonable concern, "how do we know you won't just pocket the money?"

Several of the others voiced the same concern. Longarm had no choice but to confess that he was a federal marshal, and that caused quite a bit more stir. They demanded to see his badge, and he obliged.

"Marshal," the bartender said, "you need to get some answers around here. This kind of thing is happening too often."

"I'll investigate," Longarm promised. "And I'll make sure to send that telegram to the man's family in Bisbee. Until then, you'd better get his body over to the undertaker."

Longarm was upset as he headed back to the telegraph office. He fired off a message to Bisbee, then to the marshal at Tucson and finally one to Billy Vail requesting if their agency had any information on Vince Pendergast or a man named Earl Jessup. It was a long shot that the federal agency would have an interest or knowledge about either man, but Longarm was a good lawman, and he wanted to cover all the possibilities.

When the telegrams were sent off, he said to the operator, "I heard that this wasn't the first time that Deputy Marshal Pendergast has gunned down someone."

"It happens pretty often. His boss, Marshal Yates, seems to have given him a free hand at administering justice."

"What I saw wasn't even remotely related to justice," Longarm replied. "It was a travesty. Jessup was never given a chance to surrender."

"Might have been just as well."

"What is that supposed to mean?"

The telegraph operator swallowed nervously. "I guess

I shouldn't say anything more. It isn't healthy to talk about Yates or Vince Pendergast. It ain't a bit healthy!"

"Talk," Longarm ordered.

"Well," the operator said, wiping his brow with a handkerchief, "them two live pretty well. Both like to gamble and, from what I've heard, they lose a lot of money every night in the gambling halls. There's talk that they're financing their gambling losses with what they take off victims they claim are wanted for crimes outside of Tombstone."

"Why doesn't the city council step up and make them accountable?"

"The city council doesn't do much. We've had a few well-intentioned citizens try to make changes . . . but like I said, it ain't healthy to criticize."

"Damn," Longarm whispered to himself.

"You gonna take 'em to task, Marshal Long?"

"I might just have to."

"Be careful," the telegraph operator warned. "Yates isn't anything special with a gun, but young Vince is as fast as they come, and he's cunning. He sure is a different breed than his father or sister."

"I expect so."

"I'll keep quiet. You gonna come back here and check and see if you got any answers to your telegrams?"

"I'll do that on my way out," Longarm said.

"If I hear from either Bisbee or Tucson, you can just pull up your buckboard in front, and I'll come out and hand 'em to you."

"Thanks."

"Think nothing of it," the man said. "The law in this town is rotten to the core, and changes are way overdue. I just hope that you don't get killed tryin' to make 'em."

"Me, too," Longarm said with a wry grin, as he turned and headed down the street to see if Donita was finished with her shopping. He would wait until he heard back from Tucson and Bisbee, and then, pneumonia or not, he was going to have a few words with the law about the way they were behaving in Tombstone.

Chapter 7

"I'm looking for Donita," Longarm told the owner of the small mercantile. "She was supposed to meet me here after doing her shopping."

"Oh," the balding, middle-aged man said, "she finished up here almost an hour ago."

Longarm frowned. "Do you know where I can find her?"

"And who are you?"

"I'm the fella that drove her into town," Longarm said. "Donita told me she would be ready to go about now, and I expected to find her and the supplies loaded."

The clerk was stocking cans of peaches and sardines. He frowned, looked at Longarm and said, "The supplies she ordered are loaded and under a tarp. As for the lady, you might try the Buckhorn Hotel just up the street."

Longarm didn't understand. "What would Donita be doing at a hotel?"

The clerk suddenly found something to do a few aisles away, and he took off without answering Longarm's question. That was irritating, so Longarm grabbed the smaller man by the arm.

"Hold up, mister! I just asked you a question. What

would Donita be doing at the Buckhorn Hotel?"

The man squirmed but could not break free of Longarm's powerful grip. In exasperation, he snapped, "You're a grown man, so I'd think you ought to be able to figure out yourself why a woman would go to a hotel for an hour."

Longarm felt stupid and released the store owner. "Yeah. Sorry about that."

"You shouldn't push a fella like that, mister. I try to mind my own damn business. As long as it doesn't affect me, what anyone does in Tombstone is none of my concern."

"Isn't the Buckhorn Hotel a few blocks up the street?"

"That's right." The clerk straightened his tie. "Now, if you don't mind, I'd like to get back to work."

"Sure," Longarm said, feeling guilty for having frightened and angered the grocery-store clerk. "How about opening me a can of sardines, and I'll buy some crackers to eat 'em with."

"Fine," the man said, obviously still miffed.

Longarm took his crackers and sardines outside and sat down on the boardwalk. He used the crackers to spoon out the fish and juice, and it tasted so good, he went back and bought another can and more crackers. After finishing them off, he inspected the buckboard and saw that it was loaded with supplies. Everything was in order except that Donita was missing.

Try as he might, Longarm couldn't help but wonder about her lover. Was he a respectable businessman or maybe a handsome gambler? He might be married, and he might be an eligible bachelor, and none of that was his business except that he was a naturally curious man. And the other thing was that Donita had lied to him when she'd said that it would take her a couple of hours to do her shopping. More likely, she had simply given the clerk a shopping list and then hurried over to have her lover's rendezvous.

Longarm realized he shouldn't be surprised at the deception when he considered Donita's age and attractiveness. Why, he'd been thinking that maybe he and she could strike a few sparks and maybe even have some fun back at the ranch. Now, it appeared that Donita was already having that kind of fun, and his chances with her were slim to none.

Bored, Longarm strolled up the street until he came to the Buckhorn Hotel. He glanced inside, and the only person in sight was the hotel desk clerk who was sitting in the lobby reading a newspaper. Longarm had an itch to go up to the clerk and insist on seeing Donita. But then he realized that would be unkind, because it would cause a good deal of embarrassment for Donita. Instead, Longarm walked across the street and took a chair in front of a barber shop to await her appearance.

When Donita appeared, she was flushed and looked excited. That was to be expected. What was not expected was that it was none other than Deputy Marshal Vince Pendergast who guided her out onto the boardwalk.

Longarm ducked his chin so that his face was hidden and he looked as if he were dozing. He waited a few moments, and when he looked up again, both Donita and Vince were walking about fifteen paces apart with the deputy marshal in the lead.

Longarm came out of his chair and followed Donita back to the grocery store. He waited a few moments, then went in and acted surprised to see her. "Well, hello! Sorry I'm late."

"That's all right," she said. "I think I'm a little late myself. Our supplies are loaded. Are you ready to go back to the ranch?"

Longarm glanced down the aisle at the clerk, and, as expected, the man paid them no mind. Looking back at

Donita, he said, "I need to stop by the telegraph office for a moment."

"That's fine. We pass it on our way out. I'll just sit in the buckboard while you handle your business."

When Longarm returned to the telegraph office, there were two telegrams waiting. One was from Billy Vail saying that he was glad Longarm had safely arrived in southern Arizona, and that he would check up on any felons named Earl Jessup. The second telegram was from the marshal of Tucson saying that he had never heard of Earl Jessup.

"I'll be back in a day or two, and I'm expecting to hear something from a Mrs. Jessup," Longarm quietly told the telegraph operator. "Not a word to anyone about any of this. Right?"

"Right, Marshal."

Satisfied that the man would keep his silence, Longarm went back out to the buckboard, climbed in and drove out of Tombstone without saying a word to the young woman sitting beside him.

When they had driven about halfway to the ranch, Donita said, "My, you sure are the quiet one this afternoon. Did you have a good time in town?"

"I had a couple of beers, some crackers and sardines," Longarm said.

She smiled. "You should have had something better than that to eat."

"It wouldn't have matched up to the way that you cook."

"That's a nice thing for you to say, Custis. Did you do anything else?"

Longarm considered the question, and then made his decision to broach the subject of Marshal Pendergast. "Actually," he said, "I saw a man gunned down in the Crystal Palace Saloon."

Donita's smile died. "Really?"

74

"That's right. Vince came in and shot a man standing at the bar without even giving him a warning."

She turned her head away without comment.

Longarm pushed it harder. "Vince said that the man he shot to death was a wanted man. A murderer. The man's name was Earl Jessup. That name mean anything to you?"

Donita turned. "No. Why should it?"

"Well, I was wondering if you might have met him at the Buckhorn Hotel on one of your little shopping trips into Tombstone."

Her mouth dropped, and her eyes widened with shock. "Why you . . . you were spying on me!"

Donita reared back and slapped him—hard. Tears filled her eyes and she cried, "Stop this thing!"

Longarm reined the team in, not sure what she was going to do next.

Donita jumped to the ground and started walking toward the ranch.

"Hey," he shouted. "There's no need for you to walk. We've still got at least another five miles to go."

But Donita didn't turn back to cuss him out or to say a word. Stiff-backed and obviously hurt and furious, she marched on down the dusty road toward the Tombstone Ranch.

Longarm waited a few moments, then set the buckboard in motion. It only took a few minutes before he came abreast of the fiery young woman, and he leaned towards her and said, "Look. If you and Vince are lovers, that's fine. It just took me by surprise, and I didn't much appreciate being lied to back in town."

She scrubbed tears from her eyes and glared up at him on the wagon seat. "We're not lovers!"

"Oh?" he asked, eyebrows lifting in question. "Well, what were you two doing in the hotel, playing checkers?"

"No! We were . . . oh, never mind! It's none of your business."

75

Longarm set the brake and hopped down before she could walk away. He took her arm and said, "Let's be honest with each other for a change. All right?"

"Let go of me!"

"I'm a United States marshal," he said, showing her his badge. "And I don't care if you and Vince do carry a torch for each other . . . although I think he's a dangerous and devious young man. But what *is* important is that he gunned what I believe to be an innocent man down in the Crystal Palace Saloon."

"Then why didn't you arrest him?"

"Because I wanted some information first," Longarm replied. "And I've sent telegrams off to get answers. But if you were in the hotel after the shooting with Vince, then it would be impossible for you not to know why he shot that man down."

"I don't know anything about any shooting."

"Of course you do." Longarm shook his head. "I didn't come here to get involved in trouble. I came because I need rest and fresh, warm air. But I think what I saw today was murder . . . plain and simple. And if the answers that come back to me say that Earl Jessup wasn't a killer, but instead an innocent victim, then I'll go after your lover."

"I told you that he's not my lover!"

"But you were making love in the hotel."

Fresh tears spilled down her cheeks, and she tried to turn away but he held her in his grasp. "Answer me!"

"Yes!"

Longarm released the woman. "I would have thought you had more sense than to get involved with someone like Vince Pendergast. Even his father held him in low regard. What is it? The idea that Vince might one day inherit the ranch with his sister, and you could become a part owner? Is that why you are seeing someone like that?"

"No."

76

Longarm shook his head. "Then what is it? Is he paying you well for your favors in bed?"

Donita's eyes blazed, and she swung at him again but Longarm caught her free hand. "Never mind," he said. "For some reason, I just thought better of you."

"You know nothing about me, Marshal Long!"

"I know that you lied to me so you could go to bed with Vince Pendergast. Given that, I figure I don't want to know anything more about you."

He climbed back up into the buckboard, suddenly feeling tired. "Get up here. It's stupid to walk when you can ride."

Donita's dark eyes were filled with hatred as she glared at him, but she climbed back into the wagon.

After that, they had nothing at all left to say to each other on their way back to the ranch.

Chapter 8

Donita made it a point to avoid being alone with Longarm during the next few days. Candice was busy readying things for the first of her prosperous eastern guests, and Longarm helped her as much as he could with the idea of slowly rebuilding his strength. And each evening, he and Candice went for a walk, which was always rewarded by a spectacular Arizona sunset.

"You're getting stronger and looking much better," Candice said one evening as they strolled hand in hand back toward the ranch house with the sun glowing like fire in the western sky. "It's good to see the color coming back to your cheeks."

"I didn't realize I looked that bad."

"Oh, you didn't!" Candice said quickly, then added, "Well, you sort of did."

Longarm took a deep breath, and there was still a little rattle in his lungs, but they were much clearer now. "I'm feeling better every day. When are the first of your guests arriving?"

"I never know." Candice shrugged. "The Melloncamps are usually the first, and they could show up any day now."

"If they don't let us know which train they're arriving on, how do we know when to drive up to Benson and get them?"

"We don't. Sometimes they send word ahead, but often they just arrive and send someone down here for the carriage. And, one year, they rented their own buggy and driver and showed up unexpectedly at the door."

Longarm shook his head. "Seems like an odd way for rich folks to do things."

"The very rich do things very differently," Candice said. "They can be sweet but also extremely inconsiderate. I know one thing . . . they were greatly saddened to learn about the death of my father. I received cards of condolence from every single guest family. And with some of those cards came donations that they asked to be made to a suitable charity in Father's name."

"Are the Melloncamps nice?"

Candice giggled. "I'm not sure that *nice* is the proper word. They're both amateur natural scientists and collectors."

"Collectors of what?"

"Everything! One year they were focused on collecting moths and butterflies. Another year they were intent on discovering Indian rock art and arrowheads. Everything Indian fascinated them, and we even sent for some of the Apache from over at the San Carlos Reservation. I tell you what, those Apache made more money that week selling their crafts and art than they ever made robbing a stagecoach!"

"Who else is coming?"

"Wait and see. There's an interesting collection."

They climbed up on the veranda and sat to watch the last of the dying sunset. Longarm studied Candice's face bathed in the soft glow of light and said, "I expect that you'll remarry before many more years pass."

She smiled. "What brought that to mind?"

"You're too beautiful and filled with life to live alone."

Candice squeezed his hand. "You flatter me. The truth is, I'm reasonably satisfied with my lot in life. I miss James and my father terribly, of course. The good news is that at least I'm living out here where there is so much natural beauty, and I enjoy my work taking care of guests part of the year and cattle the rest."

"This is a fine place," he said.

"Do you like it here?"

"Who wouldn't? It's a fine ranch."

"Vince wants to sell it, and I refuse."

Longarm leaned closer to Candice. "So what is going to happen?"

"I don't know," she admitted. "But Vince has gone to Tucson and hired a lawyer who sent me a letter saying that I either have to agree to a sale or else buy him out at the fair market price."

"Do you have the money to do that?"

"Not yet."

Longarm frowned, not wanting to bring up the subject of what he'd seen and learned about Vince and Donita in Tombstone. On the other hand, he had a feeling that this woman ought to know that her cook, housekeeper and friend was her brother's lover.

"Candice, when Donita and I went to Tombstone, something troubling happened."

"I sensed that," she said. "Donita was very quiet and looked upset when you returned. I was wondering if you'd tell me what went wrong on that little shopping trip."

"I was in the Crystal Palace having a beer when your brother burst into the saloon and gunned down a man named Earl Jessup."

Candice's eyes widened. "You mean Vince just shot this man?"

"That's right. He said Jessup was wanted for murder over in Tucson, but when I sent a telegram to the marshal of that town, he sent a reply back saying that he'd never heard of Earl Jessup."

"I don't know what to say."

"I'm going back to Tombstone tomorrow," Longarm told her. "I also sent a telegram to Bisbee where Jessup was supposed to have a family. If that telegram comes back, I want to find out more about Jessup and his background. Candice, your brother might have to stand trial for the murder of Earl Jessup."

She stared at him for a moment, then stood up. "I think that I need a drink. Would you care to join me?"

"I'd like that," he replied.

They went into the parlor, and Candice poured them both two generous whiskies. Longarm was considering telling this woman about Vince and Donita when Candice said, "Custis, you were right about me not being able to live alone. I need someone strong and trustworthy. Someone like you that I can lean on when trouble comes my way."

"I have broad shoulders," he said, "but I won't be here that long. Maybe you should be looking in another direction."

Candice shook her head. "I have been looking and there is no one else in sight. Do you think you could . . . could fall in love with me?"

The question caught Longarm completely by surprise. "Candice, what you don't know is that I'm a deputy United States marshal."

"No."

"It's true. I jumped into a fast-moving creek in Denver to save a drowning kid, and that's how I caught pneumonia, and why I'm here now."

"Did my father know?"

"Yes. I told him because I didn't want him to learn it second hand."

"Why didn't you tell me sooner?"

"It just didn't seem important, and I've found it best not to tell people unless there is a reason. Now there is a reason."

"Me?"

"And your brother who may have gunned down an innocent man for reasons I can't yet understand."

Candice gulped down the remainder of her whiskey and stared him in the eyes. "I'm sorry you're a federal lawman, but only because it means that you will probably want to return to your duties."

"That's right. I like being a lawman, and I'm good at the job."

"But you don't have to lock yourself into doing that forever!" She took his drink from his hand and laid it on a corner table, then wrapped her arms around his neck. "Custis, why don't you at least consider the idea of staying here with me."

"In what role?"

She kissed his mouth, and he kissed her back before she breathed, "In whatever role you want as long as you fall in love with me."

Longarm heard footsteps in the hallway, and he wondered if Donita was trying to overhear their conversation. "Is there someplace we can go to talk in private?"

"That was probably just Donita going to the kitchen. She likes to raid the pantry at all hours."

"Why don't we go up to your room?"

Candice kissed his neck, face and closed eyes. "But, if we did that, you might want to take advantage of me."

"I'm a sick man. Remember?"

"I don't think you're all that sick."

"Why don't we find out?"

"All right."

When Longarm came to his feet, and they kissed again, he realized that there was nothing sick about him below his waist. And when they went upstairs and tore each

83

other's clothes off, he had never felt healthier.

Candice turned back the bedspread, covers and her slick silk sheets, then fell back on the bed reaching for him. "This will be my first time since James died."

"I hope that . . ."

She silenced his concerns with a passionate kiss, and then arching her back slightly, Candice brought his face down to her aching breasts. Longarm paid them equal attention, and, soon, the beautiful young woman was moaning and reaching for his manhood.

"I've waited too long," she whispered, "take me quickly!"

Longarm wasn't one to question such an offer or opportunity. He climbed between her widely spread legs and plunged his stiff rod into her as far as it would go.

"Oh, Custis," she groaned, "James wasn't nearly so huge!"

"Let's not talk about him," Longarm grunted as he began to move up and down and then around and around, driving the woman into a frenzy. "Let's just enjoy this every bit as much as we can while it lasts."

Candice moaned, and he took that as agreement. And although she was slamming her hips upward and had her fingernails biting into his buttocks, urging him to a fast and violent consummation of their passion, Longarm wisely held back and worked her body as if he were a musician, and she was his instrument. He brought her up slowly to a screaming crescendo, and when she hit her highest note, he roared with his own passion and filled her body with his thick, hot seed.

The woman would not let go of him afterward. Candice held him in her arms and her legs, and he kissed away her warm, salty tears of joy.

"Can I assume it was as good for you as it was for me?" he asked.

"Oh," she whispered, "I never had any man make love

to me so long and so powerfully. I thought I was going to go crazy there at the end."

"You let out quite a scream," he said.

Candice bit her lower lip. "I hope Donita didn't hear us."

"Don't worry too much about her," he said. "Donita is no angel and she understands what it feels like to be made love to."

Candice looked up at him. "I'm sure she does, but it's odd that you should say that."

"Forget it," he said, still not ready to tell this woman about Donita and her brother until he had more information and sorted it out in his mind.

"Sleep with me tonight? Make love to me over and over? Please?"

"All right," he said.

"You could even move back into the house tomorrow and . . ."

"No," he told her. "That would compromise your reputation."

"So what!" Candice cried. "I'm falling in love with you, and I don't want to sleep alone anymore. Custis, I . . ."

He kissed her into silence, and then they held each other close until they fell asleep. But just before that happened, Longarm heard footsteps outside in the hallway, and he just knew that it was Donita . . . listening.

Chapter 9

"I'd like to saddle up one of your guest's horses and ride into Tombstone," Longarm told Candice a few days later. "I need to see if those telegrams I sent to Denver and Bisbee brought back any responses."

"Would you like me to go with you?"

"Not unless you want to," Longarm told her as they stood on the veranda and watched the cowboys ride out for a day of work on the range. "I'm sure you have plenty to do around here now that the guests are about to arrive."

"I do, but I'm worried."

"About me . . . or your brother?"

Candice sighed and took a chair. "Custis, I'm falling in love with you."

"Look," he said, not quite able to find the right words, "I'm not ready to settle into a harness."

She looked up quickly, pain filling her eyes. "Do you really think getting married would be like putting on a harness?"

"No, but . . ."

"Because if so . . . then you can just saddle up and keep riding!"

Candice started to turn and rush into the house but

Longarm grabbed her. "Listen, I never meant that I'd feel harnessed. Being your husband would be an honor. It's just that I'm used to my freedom, and I like what I do for a living."

"And maybe . . . if you gave it a chance . . . you'd also love ranching and helping me here at the Tombstone Ranch."

"I'd like to think so, but . . ."

"At least stay long enough to meet the guests and find out what we do before you make up your mind."

"All right. But I have to go to Tombstone today. Your brother made a Bisbee woman a widow. *You* ought to understand how she feels, and for all we know, Earl Jessup left children fatherless. I can't just ignore what I saw happen in the Crystal Palace Saloon. I have to find out the truth and . . . even if that means arresting your brother for murder."

"If you attempt to arrest Vince, there will be another shooting, and I don't want either of you dead. Vince considers himself a lawman. He'd never allow himself to suffer the humiliation of being arrested and locked up in his own town."

"If Jessup was an innocent man, I'll let Marshal Yates arrest your brother."

Candice shook her head. "Jessup *wasn't* an innocent man."

"How do you know?" Longarm asked, surprised by the conviction he heard in her voice. "You said you'd never heard of that man."

"I know because Vince wouldn't just shoot someone down without a good reason. He has a temper, and he can be rough, but he's not the cold-blooded killer you think he is."

Longarm didn't see that any more talk was going to clear things up, so he said, "Any particular horse I should borrow today?"

"Take that white-faced roan in the corral behind the barn. Baldy is a good, steady animal."

"What about a saddle and bridle?"

"Pick any you want in the tack room," she replied, face pinched with worry. "And Custis, if you kill my brother . . . I'm not sure that I'll be able to forgive you."

"What if he tries to kill me first?"

Candice's hands dropped helplessly to her sides. "I just don't know. Vince isn't much, but he's all the family I have left. And you don't think you could get married and settle down here at this ranch. So what does that leave me?"

"I don't know," he said, honestly.

When Longarm turned, Candice grabbed his waist and hugged him tightly. "Just be careful. Vince is an expert with a six-gun, and Marshal Yates is also extremely dangerous."

"I'll be careful," he promised, unclasping her hands and heading for the tack room to get a halter and lead rope.

Baldy turned out to be spunky and anxious to gallop because of his long seasonal layoff. Custis could feel the animal wanting to buck and lunge, but he kept the gelding on a tight rein. Longarm glanced back and saw Candice on the veranda waving good-bye, and Donita framed by an open upstairs window. Donita's arms were folded across her chest, and she was staring at him with an expression that did not warm his heart. Longarm finally gave the rambunctious gelding free rein, and the animal charged down the road like a runaway freight train. Baldy didn't stop running until he was lathered and blowing hard.

"You're as out of shape as I am," he told the roan, as it slowed to a sensible walk.

The ride into Tombstone was uneventful. Longarm met many ore wagons coming and going to the smelters, and there were also quite a few other travelers of all ages and descriptions. One was an old man in ragged clothes who looked like he was about to collapse from hunger.

"Do you have just a little charity in your heart, brother?" the man cried when Longarm overtook him just a mile out of town. "A little Christian charity for one of God's poorest children?"

"You're no child," Longarm said. "Why'd you let yourself get in such a bad fix?"

"Life isn't fair, mister. You're still young and strong. But someday you might find that cruel fate also puts you in my sad, sad circumstances. And if unlucky fate should befall you, you'll pray that some younger man will take pity and spare you a dollar."

Longarm didn't have a lot of money, but he was saddened to see an old man so abused by life. Never mind that he had most likely brought on his own fate.

"Here you go," he said, giving the beggar a silver dollar.

"Bless you, brother! May God reward you for your charity!"

"And may you spend that dollar on food, shelter or clothing and not on rotgut whiskey," Longarm said as he rode on past.

Tombstone hadn't changed much in the few days that Longarm had been gone. The town was still busy and crowded. Longarm reined his horse up in front of the telegraph office and went inside.

"Howdy," the telegraph operator said. "I got a message from Denver."

Longarm read the brief message from Billy Vail who said that there were no known arrest warrants out on Earl Jessup. "Did you hear from Mrs. Jessup?"

"She's in town. Arrived on a stagecoach a few days

ago, and the first thing she did was get the funeral collection money that you left at the bank."

"Good. Did she give her husband a nice burial?"

"Nope. She gave him a pauper's burial. In fact," the telegraph operator said, "I was talking to the undertaker, and he said she didn't even want to spend money on his cheapest wooden casket."

"Is that a fact?"

"It is. Why, she'd have had him wrapped up and buried in a woolen blanket if it hadn't been against the city's ordinance that says you have to at least plant the deceased in a simple pine box."

"Did she seem to be grieving at all over the death of her husband?"

"Nope. They said she didn't shed a tear. The Reverend Peterson offered to say a few words at the burial and read from the Holy Bible, but Mrs. Jessup told him it wouldn't be necessary. She said that her husband wasn't a Christian man, and she wasn't a Christian lady, so it would be hypocritical to have a man of the cloth go on about God and heaven. Can you believe that, Marshal?"

"Well," Custis said, "there are people like that. Did the woman go back down to Bisbee?"

"Nope. She took a job at Silver Spur Saloon, one of the roughest in town. I tell you, she's pretty, but hard as nails."

"I need to have a few words with her about her husband and his death."

"If Mrs. Jessup ain't workin' at the saloon right now, you'll probably find her at Midas Boardinghouse over on Fifth Street. That's about the only place a woman on her own can find a room."

"I'll look her up," Longarm said. "Any other messages?"

"Nope. But Vince Pendergast must have seen you come

out of here the other day because he asked me if you'd sent any telegrams."

"And you said?"

"Only one to a friend in Denver. He asked me about the message you sent, but I told him it was just about your wife and children."

Longarm had to smile. "You told him I had a wife and children?"

"Yep." The man shrugged. "I didn't know what else to say. You did order me not to tell anyone you was a federal marshal."

"That's right. Thank you for keeping that confidence."

"You can thank me by getting rid of Marshal Yates and Pendergast. They're poisoning this town. I wasn't any fan of Wyatt Earp and his brothers, but these boys are far worse."

Longarm headed for the Silver Spur to see Mrs. Jessup. He was surprised that she had not seemed upset, and her attitude created more questions and heightened his curiosity.

When Longarm stepped into the Silver Spur, he could see that it was a rough workingman's saloon. There was a raised stage over in one corner where a man was playing an out-of-tune piano very badly. Several young women were working the customers, sitting on their laps and generally showing them a good time while trying to get them to buy them watered-down drinks. It occurred to Longarm that one of the girls might be Earl Jessup's widow.

Longarm went up to the bartender and said, "I'm looking for Mrs. Jessup."

"She doesn't come on until five o'clock. You want a drink?"

"No, thanks."

"Suit yourself. What do you want with Katy?"

"That's my business," Longarm told the man as he headed out the door.

Midas Boardinghouse was a neat brick home and there were three calico cats sleeping on the porch. Longarm had to pick his way around them to reach the door.

"What do you want?" a loud, shrill voice sounded from somewhere within.

"I need to talk to Katy Jessup."

"Get lost."

Longarm continued knocking until an old woman with long gray hair tied in two pigtails and wearing a loose house dress finally opened the door and shouted in his face, "Mister, are you stone deaf?"

"No. I need to see Mrs. Jessup."

"She's still sleeping."

"Wake her up."

"Who the hell do you think you are? I don't take orders from anybody."

Longarm could see that he was going to have to try and be more pleasant. "Look," he said, "I'm a deputy United States marshal investigating the death of her husband. I *must* talk to her."

Maude studied him closely. "Let me see some identification."

Longarm showed the woman his badge, and Maude finally nodded her double chins and said, "All right. But Katy won't want to tell you anything. She had no use for her husband anyway."

"She must have thought something of him or she wouldn't have come to see that he was properly buried."

In response to that remark, Maude made a sound that was neither ladylike nor complimentary. It didn't smell too good either, causing Longarm to take a sudden back step and tromp on one of the cat's tails.

The calico howled, and all three cats scattered. Maude shook her head in disgust. "You're as big and clumsy as an ox. Probably as stupid as one, too."

Longarm's patience was at the breaking point. It was

clear that this old harridan was a man-hater. "Just go wake Mrs. Jessup up, and tell her to come out and have a few words with me."

"And if I refuse?"

"Then I'll come in and find her."

"Over my dead body!"

Longarm placed his hand on the butt of his six-gun and said in his mildest voice, "I hope that's not the case, but it's your call."

Maude blinked with surprise and retreated into the house. Longarm took a seat on the porch steps and waited. After a while, the three cats slunk back and began to demonstrate that they weren't upset with him anymore as they rubbed against his pants legs. Longarm wasn't in the mood to please cats so he decided to smoke one of his cheap cigars. That did the trick because the cats disappeared again.

"Who are you?" a voice said from just inside the front room of the brick boardinghouse.

He stood up and turned around, but Katy Jessup was standing in shadows, so he couldn't really see her very well.

"My name is Deputy Marshal Custis Long."

"Where are you from?"

"Denver."

"What could you possibly want to talk to me about?"

"Ma'am. Could I come inside? I can't even see your face."

"Maude wouldn't like that." Katy Jessup stepped outside wearing a bathrobe. She was taller than average and definitely a good-looking woman with reddish brown hair and light brown eyes that were still puffy for lack of sleep.

"I was in the Crystal Palace Saloon when Deputy Vince Pendergast shot your husband down."

"My husband and Vince had words a few months earlier in Bisbee. They fought, and Earl whipped Vince real bad. That's what the killing was all about. Are you also a lawman?"

"That's right," Longarm said, "I'm a federal marshal. Tell me why they fought."

"Earl caught me in bed with Vince . . . twice. The second time is when he beat him up so bad. If I hadn't pulled him off, he'd have killed Vince with his bare hands. And he told Vince he was going to come here to Tombstone and finish what he'd started. Earl vowed to kill Vince even if that meant that he had to ambush him on the street so that he'd never mess with another man's wife."

"That's what your husband said?"

"That's right. I knew that one or the other was going to die. I was just hoping it would turn out to be Earl, and it was."

Longarm had heard almost everything in his time, but the way this woman told him she had been cheating on her husband and wished him dead was so matter-of-fact that he was a bit taken aback.

"Did you know that Marshal Pendergast also took a roll of money and other valuables from your husband's body?"

It was the woman's turn to be surprised. "No! Are you sure?"

"Yes. I saw him."

"Why that thieving son of a . . . I'm going to find Vince, and get what's coming to me right now!"

The woman would have jumped off the porch and stormed up the street if Longarm hadn't blocked her path and said, "Why don't you get dressed, and we'll both go pay a visit to the marshal's office? I have some questions of my own I mean to ask him."

Katy Jessup nodded. "All right. But Vince wouldn't know how to tell you the truth. He's all lies and promises."

"What did he promise you?"

"That's none of your business."

"I'm making it my business. What did Vince say he'd do for you before you went to bed with him?"

"His father owns a big ranch just a ways from town. Vince said that, if I left my husband, he'd marry me, and when he inherited Tombstone Ranch, we'd both be rich and livin' real easy from then on."

"He said that?"

"That's right. What's it to you, anyway?"

Longarm shrugged. "Nothing, I guess. I was just wondering what it would have taken for you to cheat on your husband."

Katy's face hardened. "Listen, mister. Earl was always cheatin' on me. He ran around with any woman he could find and put to bed. So don't be trying to make me feel guilty. I was faithful to Earl for the first few years, but after about the fifth or sixth time I caught him cheating on me, I finally gave up and decided that what was good for the gander was gonna be good for the goose as well."

"I see." Longarm shook his head. "Go in and get dressed. I'll wait right here."

Katy studied his face. "Are you married?"

"No."

"Well," she said, "it don't matter anyway."

"Why is that?"

"Because, if you're gonna go challenge Vince, sooner or later you'll get the same medicine that Earl got in the Crystal Palace."

"I wouldn't bet on that."

"I would," she said. "If Vince don't kill you first, then Yates will finish the job."

"Let's quit flapping our mouths and go have a talk with them."

"Fine with me. I could use any money that is rightfully mine. Earl wasn't much, but he was a damn good poker player, and sometimes he'd win some big stakes. If he had money on him when he was shot, you can bet that's how it was gained."

Longarm nodded and sat down in a chair. The three calico cats appeared almost immediately and began to rub his pants legs.

"Cats like you," Katy observed. "You'll notice that they don't come slinkin' around rubbin' my legs."

"Why is that?"

"I tromp 'em and kick 'em off the porch. I don't like cats, dogs or any other pets. They're just a big nuisance. You got to feed 'em and tend to 'em and what do you get in return?"

"Your legs rubbed?"

"Ha!" Katy laughed. "If you want to get rubbed, mister, I think I can do the job a lot better than them three stupid cats!"

"Yeah," Longarm said, "I'll just bet you could at that."

"Keep it in mind," Katy Jessup said, giving him a wink before she went back into Maude's house to get dressed.

Chapter 10

It took nearly twenty minutes for Katy Jessup to get herself fixed up and ready to march down the street. Longarm figured that the pretty but calloused widow must have realized that she was not looking her best in a bathrobe and with her hair all messed up and eyes puffy from lack of sleep.

Longarm didn't care about any of that, and he wasn't sure what he would say to Vince now that he had learned that the man he'd gunned down in the Crystal Palace Saloon had openly sworn to ambush the deputy on sight. Given that knowledge, it would be unwise to arrest or charge Vince with murder. Given what Katy had told him, most frontier judges would do no more than give Vince a lecture and perhaps a stiff fine.

When they arrived at the marshal's office, Longarm opened the door to see Vince and Marshal Tom Yates playing a game of poker complete with chips and cash on the table. From the size of his pile of chips, it appeared that Vince was the big winner, but he paled slightly when he saw Katy and Longarm who said, "I understand this woman is the reason why you killed Earl Jessup in the Crystal Palace Saloon."

"Who the hell are you?" Yates demanded.

Longarm reached into his vest pocket and extracted his badge. Introducing himself, then adding, "I came to Arizona for my health, but I was there when your deputy gunned down Earl Jessup in cold blood."

"I didn't gun him down!" Vince shouted. "Earl was reaching for his derringer. The man had threatened to kill me on sight. It's not my fault that I saw him first."

"Is that the way you read it?" Longarm asked. "Because, where I come from, the law says that a man is entitled to a fair shake. If you were worried about Jessup, you should have arrested him and let a judge decide if he should be sentenced to jail or prison."

Vince laughed, but it wasn't a nice sound. "Marshal, you have no idea about how we operate in Tombstone. In case you didn't know it, we've had our share of murders and shootings, and we don't wait for the bullets to start flying in our direction."

"That's enough, Vince," Yates commanded. "I'm the boss, and I'll do the rest of the talking."

Longarm had already decided that Yates was both dangerous and arrogant. Tombstone's marshal was probably in his early thirties and his clothes were wrinkled and soiled. He wore a three-day beard and was two months late on getting a haircut. Yates had a prominent jaw and deep, close-set reptilian eyes. It was pretty plain to see that Yates figured that he could do whatever he pleased when it came to administering the law.

"So, you're a federal marshal, huh?" Yates began. "Well, we don't much care for the federal government in Tombstone."

"That may be," Longarm said, "but you're a United States territory, and you fall under the law of the land. That means . . ."

Yates cut him off by shouting. "It means that we handle our own affairs! As Mrs. Jessup could or should tell you,

100

her husband had sworn to kill my deputy on sight. Vince saw him ride into town, and he followed Jessup to the Crystal Palace. Then he took the steps necessary to protect his life and maybe that of another innocent bystander."

"What did he do with my husband's watch, jewelry and money?" Katy cried, her voice shrill with anger and accusation.

"What money?" Vince asked, feigning innocence.

Longarm growled, "The roll of money that I saw you take from Jessup's body along with his jewelry."

"All right then. I impounded it as evidence."

Longarm's voice dripped with sarcasm. "That's a new one on me. What kind of evidence?"

Yates smiled coldly. "We aren't exactly sure yet, Marshal Long. But you can rest easy on that account, because Jessup's valuables will all be kept safe at the bank until such time as this case is fully satisfied."

Longarm shook his head. "If I had my guess, I'd say that you split the money and sold off the jewelry. I've heard that you have a problem with gambling, and that the people of this town are being robbed and extorted because of your expensive gambling habit."

Both the marshal and his deputy came out of their chairs, and Longarm did not miss the fact that both placed their hands on the butts of their six-guns.

"Marshal Long," Yates said in a low, hard voice, "I don't think I like you any more than I like your employer . . . the federal government. Now, you can escort this whore out of my office and get out of my town, or you can face the consequences of your foolish accusations. Which is it to be?"

Longarm wasn't in the habit of backing down from a threat, but he wasn't anybody's fool, either. The fact of the matter was that he stood face-to-face with certain death if he didn't leave Tombstone so that he could return when the odds were more in his favor.

"All right," Longarm said. "I'm finished here for the time being."

But Katy Jessup wasn't finished. "Vince, I want my husband's money and jewelry! It belongs to me and I need it right now!"

"Get out of here," he snarled, "before I knock your damn teeth down your throat."

Before Longarm could react, Katy Jessup shrieked like a panther and leapt at the sneering deputy marshal. Her fingernails raked deep furrows down both of his cheeks that filled instantly with blood. But then Vince drew back his fist and struck her in the side of the jaw, knocking the woman down so hard her head bounced on the plank flooring.

Longarm jumped forward and grabbed the deputy by the shirtfront and backhanded him across the mouth. Vince struggled, and when Marshal Yates started to rush forward into the fight, Longarm hurled Vince into his path and drew his six-gun.

"That's enough!" he yelled. "Another step and I'll put a bullet through your belly."

Yates froze in his tracks, and Vince's hand strayed toward the gun on his hip, but the marshal clamped it with his arm, hissing, "Not now! We can deal with him later."

With his Colt revolver trained on the pair of corrupt lawmen, Longarm reached down and helped Katy up to her feet. She was dazed, and her legs didn't seem to want to support her weight. Longarm managed to get her fully upright and then his arm around her waist before he started backing them out of the door.

Yates was livid. "You've gone way too far, Long! We'll be seeing you again soon."

"I expect that you will," Longarm told the man. "And by the way, Earl Jessup wasn't wanted for any crime in Tucson. What happened in the Crystal Palace was murder, and I mean to see that it doesn't go unpunished."

"You're going to wish you'd never seen Tombstone," Vince warned. "And you'd better be off my ranch when I come to visit, or I'll see you never leave there alive."

"I'll come and go when I please."

Vince reached up and touched the blood on his cheeks. Turning his hate-filled eyes on Katy Jessup, he said, "You should have stayed in Bisbee where you belonged. After I settle up with your big friend from Denver, I'll settle up with you."

The woman, though still groggy from the blow she'd taken to her jaw, actually attempted to break free and again attack Vince. It was all that Longarm could do to restrain her and back them both out of the room and into the street.

"Settle down!" he ordered.

Katy stopped struggling and swore like a mule skinner. "I hate him!" she raged as Longarm dragged her down the street past the gawking town merchants and visitors. "I should have killed Vince when he was unarmed in my bed!"

Longarm supposed that was probably true. He managed to get Katy back to Maude's boardinghouse and calmed down.

"It's not safe for you to stay any longer in Tombstone," he told the woman whose face was beginning to swell from the hard blow she'd taken. "My advice is to go back to Bisbee."

"I'm never going back there!"

"What about your children?"

"I don't have any, and I don't want any, either!"

"Well," Longarm argued, "you can't stay in Tombstone. It's clear to me that, if you're caught, Vince will either kill you or beat you senseless. You have to leave town."

"Leave town with what?" Tears filled Katy's eyes. "I don't have any money."

"What about family or friends? There must be someone that you can turn to for help."

"You're it."

Longarm shook his head. "Not me."

"If you didn't mean to see this thing through, then you shouldn't have gotten into it in the first place," she said. "After what just happened, you can't just cut me adrift without anyone to go to or any money to help me survive."

"I'm sure that you could get a job in any saloon you wanted and earn plenty of money. There are a dozens of places like the Silver Spur within a hundred miles of where we stand."

"But . . . but I don't even have travel money."

The panic in her voice told Longarm that the woman wasn't lying. "Look," he said, "if I give you train fare money to Tucson, would you promise me to stay there or keep going west?"

"Yeah," she said without much enthusiasm. "But what about all the money that Vince stole from my husband? And his jewelry! Earl had expensive tastes and his ring was worth . . . oh, at least five hundred dollars. How can you let him keep what should belong to me?"

"I'll get the ring back and send it to you," Longarm said, tired of the wrangling.

"But I don't know where I'll be," she told him. "I might stay in Tucson, but then again I might want to move on. So I don't see. . . ."

Longarm turned and walked off a few paces thinking that this was the most difficult and obstinate woman he'd come across in a long time.

"Look," he finally said, realizing that he couldn't leave her unprotected. "You can come back to the Tombstone Ranch with me and then we can sort things out from there."

"All right," she said. "But I sure don't think that

Vince's sister is going to treat me very nice."

"Candice is a good woman," he said. "And besides, you won't be staying but a day or two, and then you'll be on the westbound train heading for Tucson."

It was late in the afternoon when the roan gelding, Baldy, weary from carrying two riders all the way back from town, finally walked into the ranch yard. Longarm and Katy were almost immediately surrounded by Candice, Donita and the cowboys.

"Who are you?" Candice asked, looking at the woman riding double behind Longarm.

"This is Katy Jessup. Your brother shot her husband in the Crystal Palace Saloon."

Candice reached up and helped the woman from Bisbee off the back of the roan gelding. "You've been hurt."

"Yeah," Katy said. "Your brother popped me a hard one in the face but I got back at him good. Raked both his cheeks and drew blood."

Candice took a backward step. "Vince hit you?"

"He sure did, and he swore he would kill me sooner or later. He swore he'd kill Custis, too."

"Is that right?" she asked.

Longarm nodded. "I'm sorry to tell you this, but I'm sure that both he and Marshal Yates are corrupt."

"What are you going to do?"

"I'll go back into Tombstone in a few days and start asking questions. Then, if I get the answers I expect, I'll arrest and jail both your brother and Marshal Yates."

Candice shook her head. "You wouldn't stand a chance against them."

"Oh," Longarm told her, "I usually accomplish what I set out to do, so don't give up on me so quick."

"Custis, you're a fool." She scrubbed tears from her eyes. "And given what you plan to do, I'm going to have to ask you to leave the ranch."

105

"Are you sure that's what you want?"

Candice nodded, and then she turned on her heels and went back into the house, leaving Longarm, Katy and the cowboys standing in an awkward silence.

Donita came forward and said, "You both must be very tired and hungry. I'm sure that Miss Pendergast wouldn't mind if you waited until tomorrow to leave."

"That's not the way I read it," Longarm said.

"Please stay at least for this night. She sometimes says things that she does not mean. I will talk to her. Maybe she will change her mind."

Katy said, "I ain't one to stay where I'm not wanted. If the high and mighty Miss Pendergast doesn't want me here, then I'm leaving."

"You are hurt and very tired. It will be dark soon," Donita said. "You should stay, and maybe things will be different in the morning."

Longarm was dog tired. He had suffered several coughing fits on the way both into and out of town, and now he felt weak and badly in need of rest. "Look, Katy. Donita is right. We'll stay here until tomorrow, and then I'll have a talk with Candice. If she still feels the same about us leaving, then we'll get a ride down to Bisbee."

"And then what?"

"I'm not sure, but I'll figure out something."

"As soon as Vince and Marshal Yates find out we're in Bisbee, they'll come looking to put an end to us both."

"That would be a fatal mistake."

"For a man who doesn't look too healthy, you talk a good game."

"I'm a law officer, Katy. Those two might wear badges, but they're pretenders as far as I'm concerned. So let's just get a good night's sleep, and see what happens tomorrow."

Katy didn't look happy about staying, but Longarm

could see that she was nearly as tired as himself, so she nodded her head in reluctant agreement.

"I'll bring some food out to your cabin," Donita offered.

"I'm tired but not very hungry," Longarm told her.

"You need to eat in order to regain your health," Donita said as she headed back to the ranch house. "I'll make something delicious."

"Who is she?" Katy asked.

"The cook and one of Candice's housekeepers."

"I like her better than Miss Pendergast."

Longarm didn't have anything to say about that, so he headed for the cabin where he'd been staying, wanting nothing more than to close his eyes and sleep. He was disappointed in the way things had gone in Tombstone, but not sure what to do about it. One thing was certain, the law in that town was totally corrupt.

Chapter 11

When they entered the cabin, Katy looked around and nodded with approval at the nice curtains, expensive rugs and furniture. "Not bad," she said. "Nicer than any place I've ever slept before."

"Didn't you have your own home in Bisbee?"

"Naw. Earl was always gone, and he'd have had me live in a run-down hotel. Once I realized that he couldn't be counted upon, I worked two jobs and saved enough money to buy a little house just outside of town. It wasn't much, but I tried my best to make it look nice . . . until it burnt down. But the truth is, my house looked pretty shabby compared to this cottage. I don't ever care to go back."

"The Easterners who come as ranch guests expect things to be nice. Candice let me put up here for a while, but that seems to have come to an abrupt end."

"What did you expect?" Katy said with a shrug of her shoulders. "You're out to put her brother in prison."

Before he could reply, Longarm was seized by a coughing fit. It wasn't as severe as the ones he'd had earlier, but it still sounded bad and it left him pale and shaky.

"Katy," he said, going over to the bed. "I'm going to kick off my boots and take a nap."

"Here," she told him, "let me help."

Longarm didn't argue. His boots were tight and always a struggle to remove, so he laid back and let Katy wrestle them off his feet. Then he carefully removed his gun and holster and placed them beside him on the floor.

"Go to sleep," she ordered. "When Donita brings the food, I'll wake you up."

"Don't bother. I'll eat later."

"Are you sure?"

"Yeah. I'm really bushed."

"Then at least I don't have to worry about you trying to climb on me in the night."

"You're right about that. But I won't promise to be an honorable gentleman for two nights in a row."

Katy knew he was teasing and laughed. "We'll see how it goes tomorrow, and take things from there. Okay?"

"Sure," he told her a moment before he drifted off to sleep.

Longarm was awakened in the night by Katy who was clawing and thrashing around on the bed.

"Katy! Are you all right?"

She wasn't all right. Katy was gagging and choking. Longarm sat up fast and grabbed the young woman by her shoulders. He shook her hard, and when she suddenly went limp, he sat down, dropped her over his knee and began to pound on her back in order to dislodge whatever was blocking her windpipe.

"Come on, girl! Come on and breathe!"

When the pounding didn't work, Longarm pulled Katy to her feet and tried to shake her back into consciousness.

"Katy!"

Longarm did everything he could think of to get the young woman breathing again, but his efforts failed. After

110

ten desperate minutes, he eased her limp body back down on the bed, feeling terrible that he hadn't been able to save the young woman's life. What had she choked on?

A kerosene lamp flickered on a table where two plates of food had been delivered to their cottage. One of the plates was empty, and the other had grown cold. Longarm saw boiled potatoes and chunks of beef covered with a dark, congealed gravy. There were also slices of bread and cheese, along with a quartered apple. Katy could have choked to death on the apple or the beef. *Hell,* he thought miserably, *she could have also have choked to death on the potatoes or bread.*

Longarm rested his head in his hands for a moment. This was a totally unexpected tragedy. Katy Jessup had been hard-bitten, but she'd also possessed goodness, and Longarm was devastated that she had died so young and in such agony.

Now what was he going to do? Take her back to Tombstone and make sure that she was buried properly? She'd told him she didn't ever want to return to Bisbee, so he guessed she wouldn't mind being put to rest in Tombstone.

"I need a drink," he muttered to himself. "And there's only one place I know to get one that is close."

Longarm covered Katy with a blanket. As he passed the table, he grabbed the uneaten dinner plate and emptied it outside on the ground, figuring that one of the many ranch dogs would find and enjoy it soon enough. He went to the ranch house and entered the dark downstairs, then groped his way to the late William Pendergast's library and liquor cabinet.

He lit a lamp and found a crystal goblet, then filled it to the brim with an excellent brandy. Longarm's eyes happened to land on a box of cigars, and he helped himself to one of those as well. Lighting the cigar and inhaling only slightly in order not to set off another fit of coughing, he sipped the brandy until it was gone, and then he poured himself a second glass.

It was probably about two o'clock in the morning when he heard the stairs protesting under someone's weight, and Longarm knew that he was about to have a visitor. He wondered if it would be Donita or Candice. Or maybe the other maid who seemed to be a somewhat mysterious figure that he'd only caught glimpses of a couple of times while in this house.

"What are you doing in here?" Candice asked quietly, as she appeared in the doorway dressed in a white lace nightgown that left little to the imagination.

"I'm helping myself to your father's excellent brandy and cigars."

Her voice took on an edge. "What gives you the right to enter this house without my permission? I was very clear that you were no longer welcome."

"Candice," he said, "you might want to sit down and share a drink with me."

"Not very likely."

"Just a few hours ago," Longarm said, unable to hide his sadness, "Katy Jessup choked to death."

"No!" She had to steady herself against the door.

"It's not the kind of thing I would joke about. Why don't you sit down, and I'll pour you a brandy."

Candice walked unsteadily across the room and collapsed onto an overstuffed couch. "First my father, and now Katy. I can't believe how everything is turning out so bad!"

"Katy died hard," Longarm told her. "I tried to clear out whatever was lodged in her throat, but failed."

Candice covered her face in her hands and wept. Longarm went over to her side and held her close for several minutes.

"I think I'm cursed . . . or this ranch is cursed. Maybe both," Candice said brokenly. "What's going to happen

112

next? I'm genuinely afraid for myself and my guests. And you, with all your accusations and wanting to put my brother in prison. Where can I turn?"

"It's going to work out all right," Longarm told her, trying to sound confident. "Misfortune usually runs in streaks. That seems to be what's happening here and now."

Candice hugged him tightly. "My first guests are due any day now, and I can't guarantee their safety. I wouldn't blame them if they turned tail and ran for their lives!"

"Be reasonable," Longarm said. "Katy choked on her food, and your father had a heart failure in his advanced years."

Candice nodded. "I know that, but . . ."

Longarm handed her his glass of brandy and poured himself another. He sat down beside the distraught woman and said, "I know this seems like an ongoing nightmare, but it's going to pass."

"When?"

"I don't know."

"When you kill Vince . . . or he kills you?"

"I don't know."

"Well that's what is going to happen if you're still here the next time he shows up . . . and he *will* show up, Custis." She shuddered. "So shall I tell one of my cowboys to dig *two* graves?"

Longarm shook his head. "I'll see that she gets a Christian burial in Tombstone."

"Yes," Candice said. "That would be best."

"And then I'll just not come back."

"I want you to come back."

"No, you don't," he said. "Not as long as I believe that your brother murdered Jessup. I found out that he had threatened to ambush Vince, but that still doesn't make what happened in the Crystal Palace Saloon right. A lawman is supposed to arrest dangerous men, not gun them

113

down without even giving them the chance to surrender."

"Vince isn't a choir boy, Custis. He's hard, and he's dangerous. But, if he says that Earl Jessup was intending to kill him, then I believe that, and it does make a difference."

"Yeah, I suppose."

"Maybe you should go on to Tucson," Candice said, sounding discouraged. "That is where you had originally intended to stay and rest. Isn't it?"

"Yes."

"Then, as much as I want you to stay . . . and as much as I'll miss you when you're gone . . . perhaps it's the only solution."

"I'll give it some consideration," Longarm told her, knowing that he was going to go back to Tombstone, and either get rid of Yates and Vince Pendergast, or die trying.

"Good," she said, sipping the brandy. "And, in a few weeks or months, when everything changes, maybe you could come back and meet some of the guests and think about my offer."

"You still want to marry me?"

"I think so. I don't know. Everything I thought I wanted is turning out upside down."

"Give it some time," he said, coming to his feet. "I think I'll go out to the barn, and see if I can hitch up a buggy. It might be best if I got Katy out of here before the men wake up and realize that someone else has suddenly died."

"I'll help you," Candice told him. "Just give me a minute to go upstairs and get fully dressed."

When she was gone, Longarm tried to get the picture of Katy choking to death out of his mind. He'd seen a man choke to death before, but never a woman. In both cases, it had been a violent and scarring experience. It would take some time to clear his head of what he'd seen this night.

When Candice came tiptoeing back down the stairs, she nodded that she was ready. Together, they went out into the moonlit yard and headed for the barn.

"I'll catch up the horse, and you wait by the buckboard," Candice said. "We can hitch it up, and then you can drive it around to the cottage. I'll put a tarp in back, and when have taken poor Missus Jessup to the undertaker, you can leave the wagon at Boston's Livery. He's a friend, and he'll see that it and the horses are eventually returned."

"How will you explain the missing buckboard and two horses to your cowboys?"

"I don't have to explain anything," she told him.

They got the team hitched up, and Longarm drove the buckboard over to the cottage he and Katy had used. He went inside and wrapped her body in a blanket, then carried her outside and laid her gently in the back of the buckboard.

"What's that horrible sound?" Longarm asked.

Candice shook her head. "I don't know. But it's awful, isn't it?"

"It sounds like . . ."

And then, Longarm suddenly realized why Katy had died, and why a dog was about to suffer the same horrible fate. Katy hadn't choked to death any more than the dog they could hear in the brush that was suffering so terribly.

Longarm ran toward the sound, and Candice followed. Tearing through the brush, he finally came upon the stricken and dying animal.

"Oh my gawd!" Candice cried. "What's wrong with poor Rex?"

"He's been poisoned by a plate of food I tossed out tonight," Longarm told the woman. "Did you . . . did you have anything to do with the kitchen tonight?"

"No! Donita and Maura cooked as usual." Candice took a backward step. "Custis, are you thinking that. . . ."

"If you didn't add poison to the plates of food that were delivered to my cottage tonight, then either Maura or Donita is guilty of murdering Katy and perhaps even your poor father."

Candice shook her head back and forth. "I can't believe that!"

Longarm spun on his boot heel and jabbed a finger at the dog as it shuddered and died. "You'd better believe it," he said, his voice shaking with rage. "Someone is poisoning people here, and, if I hadn't fallen asleep before those plates of food arrived, I'd be just as dead as that poor dog!"

Longarm was pretty sure that Candice was not a murderer. That left Donita and the mysterious Maura, and he meant to arrest one or the other for murder. "Let's go to the house, and I'll have a talk with your cook and housekeeper."

"But Maura is old, and neither one of them would have any reason to poison poor Katy or my father."

Longarm was already heading back to the ranch yard. He twisted his head around to say something to Candice, and suddenly felt the searing white heat of the bullet as it struck him in the head. His legs buckled, and then he was falling into a deep, dark and bottomless abyss.

Chapter 12

·

Custis awoke with a terrible headache and the vision of Candice leaning over his face. "What happened?"

"You were ambushed last night. Thank heavens you turned your head just as the shot rang out."

He touched the bandage over his right ear. "Who did it?"

Candice shook her head. "I don't know, but you must have been right about Donita, because she was gone when we finally got you into the house."

Longarm sat up feeling as if his head were a blacksmith's anvil and someone was beating on it with a hammer. "What about your other housekeeper and cook?"

"Maura is still here."

He glanced at the window and realized it was broad daylight. "Have I been unconscious since late last night?"

"Yes. How are you feeling now?"

"I've felt better," he told her as he swung his boots from the bed. "I want to talk to Maura right now."

"I thought you might. I'll go get her. But please be gentle because she is easily upset. She came from Ireland, and the poor dear is as timid as a mouse."

"I'll try not to upset her," Longarm promised.

When Maura entered the room, Longarm studied the woman for a moment. At first glance, Maura was as plain as a board fence. But when you looked a little closer, it was easy to see that Maura was actually a comely woman, probably in her early thirties. She did appear to be shy, and, when she was told to have a seat, she kept her eyes down and fixed on her hands, which were tightly clasped in her lap. Maura wore no makeup and a faded house dress with her reddish brown hair pulled back severely in a bun.

"Miss . . ."

"Killian," Candice said.

"Miss Killian," Longarm began. "Where were you last night when the meal for me and Miss Jessup was prepared?"

Her hands became even busier, and she stared at them as if they had a mind of their own. "I was in my room, sir."

"When you answer my questions, look me in the eye, please."

Maura raised her head.

"Now," Longarm continued. "You say that you were in your room. Why weren't you in the kitchen?"

"Because," she replied, "it was Donita's day to do work in the kitchen. My job on Wednesday is always to clean the house and pay particular attention to the drapes and rugs."

"That's correct," Candice said. "We have a set schedule around here, and yesterday was Donita's turn to do the meals and clean up the kitchen."

Longarm nodded with understanding. "Miss Killian," he said, "when was the last time you saw Donita?"

The Irish woman's brow knitted with concentration. "It was about four o'clock. I finished my cleaning and went up to my room."

"Where did you eat your supper?"

"In my room."

"At what time?"

"About . . . oh, six o'clock."

"Well, you must have gone down to the kitchen to get it."

"Yes, sir, I did. But Donita was not in the kitchen, so I helped myself to a plate and took it up to my room."

"And you didn't come out at all?"

"Only when I awoke in the night at the sound of the gunshot. Then I rushed downstairs and into the yard. That's when I saw you on the ground, and everyone in a stir. I helped bring you up to this room."

"I see. Were you close to Donita?"

"Close?"

"I mean, were you good friends."

She made a face. "No, sir. We worked together, but that is all we did together. She and I were very different, and we did not talk much except about the work at hand."

"Did she seem especially nervous yesterday?"

"No."

"And you don't know when she left this ranch?"

"I think she left in the night."

Longarm leaned closer. "Why do you think that?"

"Well," Maura said, "Donita must have left in the night because she prepared the meals last evening, and she wasn't here this morning. When else could she have disappeared?"

"Exactly," Longarm said.

"I am sorry Miss Jessup and poor Rex were poisoned," Maura told him. "I very much liked that dog, and that is a terrible way to die."

"Did Donita ever say she had family or friends?"

"No, sir."

Longarm glanced over at Candice with a questioning look. The woman shook her head. "Donita was a very private person. I'm sure that she must have had some

119

friends or family in Arizona, but she never told me about them."

"Are there any horses missing?"

Candice blinked. "You know, things have been so crazy that I never thought to have the cowboys look."

"I'll go ask your cowboys," Longarm said. "She couldn't have just walked to Tombstone or up to Benson. Either she took a horse or she was picked up by the man that tried to kill me."

Candice touched his arm. "And you're already convinced that man was my brother."

"I didn't say that."

"But it's what you're thinking."

Longarm was in no mood to play word games. "Yeah," he admitted. "I think that the one who shot me was either your brother . . . or Marshal Yates."

"You could be very wrong."

"I know that," Longarm answered. "But I mean to find Donita and . . . when I do . . . I'll have some answers."

Longarm went out to the corral and found Bob. "Are any horses missing?"

The cowboy nodded and said, "As a matter of fact, I was just about to come up to the house and tell Miss Pendergast that we are missing a buckskin named Jake."

"And a saddle?"

"That's right."

"Could you track Jake?"

Bob was smoking a cigarette. Blue smoke trailed out of his nostrils when he nodded. "Jake is a big horse and he toes in on his front feet."

"You mean he is pigeon-toed?"

"You could say that."

"Why don't we see if we can pick up Jake's tracks."

"I already picked 'em up," Bob told him. "Someone rode that horse toward Tombstone."

"How far did you follow the tracks?"

Bob dropped his cigarette into the dust and ground it under his boot heel. "Not far."

"Hitch up the buckboard. I mean to take Missus Jessup to town for a burial."

"Yeah, Miss Pendergast told us she was dead. Damn shame. Same for what someone did to Rex. He was a fine cowdog."

"Let's get moving."

"Sure thing. You want me to drive the buckboard?"

"I'd appreciate that."

"If Miss Pendergast will allow me to go, I'll do it," Bob said, eyes fixed on Longarm's bandage. "But, Marshal, are you sure you're up to a long wagon ride?"

"I'm up to it."

The cowboy nodded and headed for the barn. Longarm went back to the cottage and saw that Katy's body had not been disturbed. He shook his head, feeling rage boiling up inside. No doubt that the poison had really been meant for himself but poor Katy had been the unwitting victim. Someone was going to pay for this, and he'd just bet that someone had also poisoned old William Pendergast. The real question now was *who* and *why*?

The buckskin gelding's tracks headed south for Tombstone, but the pigeon-toed horse was not joined by any others. That meant that Donita had probably been the one who had ambushed and tried to kill Longarm as well as being poor Katy's murderer.

"What do you know about Donita and Maura?" Longarm asked the cowboy as they rolled steadily south toward Tombstone.

"I know that Maura is a good woman."

"And Donita?"

Bob shook his head. "I was taught not to say bad things about folks . . . especially women. Donita was . . . well, hard."

121

"In what way?"

"Several of the young cowboys tried to impress her, and she ridiculed 'em. And by that, I don't mean just ignored their attentions, but mocked 'em so they felt bad."

"Was she meeting someone in Tombstone?"

Bob was slow to answer. "I expect that she was."

"And who was that someone?"

"My guess would be Deputy Vince Pendergast."

Longarm nodded in agreement. "It all fits," he said. "And I think that when I find Donita, I'll find Vince."

"Finding them might be the easy part," the cowboy warned. "Vince is mighty good with a six-gun, and he and Marshal Yates are the law in Tombstone. Not that you aren't also the law, but . . . well, they hold the winning cards."

"That's one way of putting it."

"I'm not armed, and, even if I was, I can't hit the side of a barn with a pistol," Bob told him.

"How are you with a shotgun?"

"I guess I could do."

"I might need your help. Will you give it?"

"Against Marshal Yates and Vince?"

Longarm nodded.

"I dunno," Bob said, looking doubtful. "I've worked at the Tombstone Ranch for many years, and I don't want to get crossways with Vince or Miss Pendergast. So, if you don't mind, I'd just as soon drop you and Miss Jessup's body off at the undertaker's, turn this buckboard around and head for home."

"I understand," Longarm told the cowboy. "And that's fine."

"I'm sorry I can't help you."

"That's okay. Sometimes it's better just to do a job by yourself than to have someone who either doesn't want to help . . . or will cause you even more problems."

"I agree," Bob said, looking relieved. "I've had men

show up at the ranch and talk Miss Pendergast into giving them a job cowboying only to learn that they don't know squat about cows or horses. Then they can be a whole lot more trouble than they're worth."

They followed the horse named Jake's hoofprints right into Tombstone before they were obliterated by the town's wagon, horse and foot traffic. Bob drove the buckboard to the front of the undertaker's office, and, with Katy wrapped in a tarp, their arrival caused a good deal of curiosity.

"Who else died out at the Tombstone Ranch?" a man blurted, his eyes fixed on the body rolled up mummylike in the tarp.

Longarm ignored the question and the growing crowd's morbid curiosity. "Bob," he said, "let's get her inside."

"It's a woman!" a big-bellied man who had overheard Longarm shouted to the others. "By gawd, they've brought in a dead woman!"

This caused even more excitement but Longarm and Bob ignored the crowd as they carried Katy inside, slamming the undertaker's door in their wake.

"Gentlemen!" said a tall, distinguished-looking man with a handlebar mustache, rubbing his soft white hands together with professional anticipation. "Who do we have here?"

"It's Mrs. Katy Jessup," Longarm answered. "She needs a proper but inexpensive burial."

The undertaker's ingratiating smile slipped quite badly. "How 'inexpensive'?"

"Under twenty dollars."

The undertaker threw up his long arms in supplication. "But, sir, my least expensive casket costs that much, and the modest fee for my own services will cost . . ."

Longarm showed the indignant mortician his badge. He

estimated he was down to less than fifty dollars, so he said, "Provide Mrs. Jessup a good and proper burial, and I'll try to get the government to pay any reasonable charges over twenty dollars."

The undertaker reluctantly nodded in agreement. He turned back the tarp to study Katy's contorted and bluish face and his eyes widened slightly. Looking up, he asked, "She looks ghastly. What on earth was the cause of her untimely demise?"

"Food poisoning," Longarm told the man.

The undertaker made a face and shook his head. "What an absolute pity. She was a rather good-looking young woman."

"Yes, she was," Longarm agreed, digging twenty dollars out of his wallet. "I'll be back to see her before she is buried."

"And what about the usual church services?"

"No services," Longarm told the man. "Just bury her well and bury her deep."

Longarm went outside and faced a crowd that numbered at least thirty. "You folks can all go back to your own business."

"Who died?" someone yelled. "Was it Mrs. Pendergast or Donita?"

Longarm didn't see any need to be evasive. Everyone would learn the answer to that question the minute he left the scene, and they flooded into the undertaker's establishment. "It was Mrs. Katy Jessup."

That surprising revelation caused quite a stir because some of the crowd remembered her from the time she had worked in the Silver Spur Saloon.

"How'd she cash it in? And what happened to your head?" another man shouted.

Longarm frowned. "Miss Jessup died of food poisoning and I . . . well, let's just say that I got lucky."

"Lucky?"

"That's right," Longarm said loud enough for everyone to hear. "Someone tried to ambush me last night, but their aim was a little off, and now I mean to find out who that person was and see that they go to jail for a long time."

He studied their faces. "Have any of you seen Donita today?"

Everyone solemnly wagged their heads.

"Has anyone seen Deputy Vince Pendergast?"

Again, no one had.

Longarm turned and headed up the street toward the marshal's office. He tore the bandage off his head and rubbed his hands together with the expectation that he might well have to draw his six-gun in a helluva big hurry.

Chapter 13

Longarm headed straight for the marshal's office, and when he stepped inside, his hand was close to the butt of his gun.

Marshal Yates was alone and he was caught by surprise. "What do you want?"

"I'm looking for a Donita," Longarm replied. "And I think your deputy knows where I can find her."

"I don't know what you're talking about," Yates said, his face suddenly flushed with anger. "And I'll tell you another thing, you're way out of line here. You have no jurisdiction and . . ."

Longarm knew that there was no sense in arguing with this man, who was as crooked as a sidewinder. "I'm going to see that you're thrown out of office before I'm through here," he told the marshal. "But first, I'm going to find Donita and your deputy and charge them both with murder. And it wouldn't surprise me one damned bit if you were right up to your eyes in this poisoning business."

Yates lost control. Longarm saw it in his eyes, and before the lawman went for the gun on his hip, Longarm drew his own pistol and cocked back the hammer in one smooth, swift motion.

"Don't do it," he warned.

Yates hadn't even cleared leather, and now his hand froze at his side. "Are you going to shoot me?" he asked, in a voice that betrayed his fear.

"No," Longarm told the man. "But if you try to follow me or in any way oppose my investigation, I'll come back and make sure that you never draw another breath."

Yates slowly nodded his head with understanding.

"Where are Vince and Donita?"

"I haven't seen Vince since yesterday. I haven't seen that woman since last week."

"Where would they be hiding?"

"Look," the marshal of Tombstone began, "you're barking up the wrong tree."

"Am I?" Longarm asked. "Or could it be that you're as guilty of murder as they are?"

Yates cursed and sat down hard in his chair. "You're headed for a bad fall, Marshal Long. You've stepped into muddy water that is way over your head."

"I can swim," Longarm told the man. "And I'm going to find Vince and Donita. If you help me, I'll keep it in mind. If not, after I deal with those two, you're at the top of my list."

Yates placed his hands on his desk. Without looking up at Longarm, he said in a quiet voice, "They often meet at a little mining shack just about a mile south of town."

"This entire area is filled with mines and shacks," Longarm told the man. "I'll need a better description."

"Their shack is about two hundred yards to the right of the road, and it rests under a hill that has two bores in it that will remind you of eye sockets. You can't miss it."

"And that's where they are?"

"That would be my best guess. They're not in town," Yates said. "I know that for certain."

"I hope you're not lying to me," Longarm told the man. "Because, if you are . . ."

"Listen, for all I know, they may have headed for Mexico or parts unknown."

"Did they also kill Mr. Pendergast?"

"Why don't you ask them?"

"I will," Longarm replied before he headed out the door. He spotted Bob sitting in the buckboard in front of the undertaker's office. The cowboy was surrounded by a crowd, so Longarm went over to the wagon.

Bob saw him at once, and the conversation died. Longarm climbed up into the wagon and said, "I need a lift down south."

"I . . . I ought to be heading back to the ranch. Miss Pendergast will be needing things done and . . ."

"Bob, it's only about a mile, and I'm not inclined to walk that far so let's stop jawin' and go."

"Okay."

The cowboy backed the team, then turned them south. They passed through Tombstone without exchanging a word, and when they were clear of the town, Longarm searched for the hill that would mark where they needed to leave the road.

"Where are we goin'?" Bob finally asked.

"Marshal Yates tells me that Donita and Vince meet at a little mining cabin just up the road a piece." Longarm raised his hand and pointed. "There's the hill he described. That must be the shack where I hope that we'll find them."

"Marshal, I sure don't want any part of this," Bob nervously fretted. "Vince is a marksman and I ain't even armed!"

"You don't need to be," Longarm said. "Just pull off the road and wait while I go to the mining shack. If there's trouble, it'll come my way . . . not yours."

"But . . ."

"Just do what I tell you."

"All right," Bob said. "But if you get killed, don't look

for me to take on Vince because I wouldn't stand a chance."

"Fine," Longarm snapped. "If I get killed, you can do whatever you damn well please, and I won't try to stop you."

"Fair enough," Bob said, missing Longarm's laconic sense of humor.

When they reached the point where a wagon track turned off the main road toward the mining shack under the hill, Longarm told Bob to pull up. He looked down and said, "I see fresh hoofprints. Bob, if it wouldn't be sticking your neck out too far, would you say they toed in and that the animal that made them is pigeon-toed?"

The cowboy craned his neck and nodded. "That's Jake's track all right. But I don't see any sign of that gelding."

"He's probably tied out of our sight between the mining shack and that hill," Longarm said, climbing out of the cabin.

"Are you just going to walk up to the shack?"

"How else would I do it?"

"Well, if Vince is inside with Donita, he may take a notion to stick his gun out the door and shoot you down."

"He might," Longarm said. "But I'm hoping that he's preoccupied with Donita."

Bob studied the shack in silence. "Maybe you should try to sneak around behind," he finally said.

The sun was going down and Longarm was running out of time, energy and patience. "No, I'm going to get this over with. Just don't leave me stuck out here."

Longarm headed up the dirt track through the sage toward the mining shack. There was no sign that anyone was inside, but he had a feeling that he'd find Vince and Donita, and he hoped they would be locked in a passionate lover's embrace.

The distance wasn't far, just a couple hundred yards as

Marshal Yates had described, but it seemed much farther. Halfway to the shack, Longarm drew his Colt. His eyes measured the cover on either side of the track, and, at each step, he was making a decision on where he'd dive if Vince Pendergast suddenly opened fire either from the doorway or the single window opening covered by a faded burlap sack.

Every muscle was taut, and Longarm prayed that he would not have a coughing fit before he reached the shack. All around him were other abandoned claims littered with rusting mining equipment, tin cans and bottle shards that glittered like silver in the dying sun.

Finally, he was at the door. Longarm took a deep breath, then leaned back, kicked it open and charged inside.

The cabin's interior was dim, and he hit the floor expecting a bullet. But there was no bullet, and there was no Vince Pendergast. Instead, he found Donita lying naked on a straw mattress with the bone-white handle of a large knife protruding from her chest. Longarm crawled over to examine the body and quickly realized that rigor mortis had set in and that the woman had been dead for at least four or five hours.

A thick horde of horseflies buzzed over the body, and it made Longarm want to choke. He backed away, climbed to his feet and went around behind the cabin. The buckskin named Jake had been tied behind there, but now it was gone. In the fading light, Longarm trailed the distinctive hoofprints away from the shack and saw that they were heading south towards maybe Bisbee or Old Mexico.

Longarm swallowed his disappointment and went back around to the front of the shack. Off in the distance, Bob was still sitting in the wagon, and Longarm motioned for the Tombstone Ranch cowboy to drive forward. Bob hesitated, but when Longarm waved impatiently and yelled, the cowboy must have realized he had no choice but to do as he was ordered by a federal lawman.

"Did you find 'em?" Bob asked when the buckboard came to a stop.

"I found Donita."

Bob looked warily at the silent shack. "What about Vince?"

"He's gone, and so is Jake."

"What about Donita?"

"We'd better go in and load her up in the buckboard."

Bob's eyes widened with horror. "Vince *killed* her?"

"She was stabbed right through the heart."

The cowboy looked like he had swallowed a frog and was about to toss it up along with whatever else was in his craw. "Marshal," he stammered, "I just don't think I can bear to handle two dead women in one day."

"Climb down, because I'm not up to carry her out by myself."

"I could go back to Tombstone and get some help."

Longarm's patience snapped. "Dammit, Bob, let's get Donita out of this mining shack and to the undertaker!"

The cowboy climbed down and followed Longarm into the shack. When Bob heard all the flies buzzing over the naked corpse, he staggered and took a back step. Longarm grabbed and yanked him forward. This was probably the most squeamish cowboy he'd ever come across. Usually they were hard and tough-minded men, well accustomed to disease and death.

"There's a blanket on that mattress. It's not as good as a tarp, but it will have to do. Let's get this over with."

Bob didn't want to get near the body. He closed his eyes, wiped his brow and shuddered, but he did help and, together, he and Longarm dragged Donita outside. They were followed by the swarm of angry flies, and the two horses pulling the buckboard tried to bolt and run, but Bob grabbed them in time.

"Oh man," the cowboy protested, blowing hard through his nose like a wind-broken horse. "I sure do hate to see this kind of thing!"

"Shut up, and let's get her into the back of the wagon."

When they'd accomplished that grisly task, and Longarm had removed the murder weapon, he spent a few unpleasant minutes searching for anything that would tie Vince to this murder. Fortunately, he found the stubs of two cigars of the same make that Vince smoked. He also found a bloodstained note in Donita's dress.

"Is this Vince's knife?"

"Never seen it before."

Longarm carefully unfolded the note.

"What's it say?" Bob asked.

Longarm didn't answer. The note wasn't signed, but said that Donita should meet the writer here and that she should tie her horse out of sight behind the shack.

Longarm studied the handwriting. He would find something written by Vince and see if the handwriting samples matched. Perhaps that wouldn't hold up in front of a judge and jury, but it would give *him* all the proof *he* needed that Vince was the man who had killed Donita and had probably tried to ambush him last night at the ranch.

"Let's get out of here," Longarm told the uneasy cowboy.

"That suits me down to the ground."

It was dark by the time they returned to Tombstone, but their arrival with a second body created even more of a crowd than when they'd delivered Katy.

"Oh my heavens!" the undertaker exclaimed when he unwrapped the body and saw Donita. "Not another one!"

"I'm afraid so."

The undertaker placed the back of his hand to his brow, and Longarm thought the man was going to swoon.

"Same deal," he said.

"And where is your twenty dollars?"

Longarm handed over the money. "Don't bury her yet," he said. "Miss Pendergast might want to have her buried on the ranch."

"She won't last long in this heat. She's already starting to bloat."

"I know."

Longarm went outside and found Bob sitting in the wagon telling the crowd about how they'd found Donita's nude and violated body.

"Bob?"

He swung around. "Yeah?"

"It's time for you to go back to the ranch. Tell Candice what happened and that I'll be staying over here tonight."

"You going to take up Vince's trail in the morning?" a stranger asked, telling Longarm that Bob hadn't given away that information.

Longarm didn't answer. Instead, he headed back to the marshal's office, but quickly discovered that it was closed. For a moment, he considered hunting Yates down and confronting him about Donita's death, and then demanding to see a sample of Vince's handwriting. There would almost certainly be one somewhere in the man's office. But Longarm just wasn't up to that tonight, so he headed for the Crystal Palace Saloon and a bottle of whiskey. After a day like this, he needed more than one drink to rid himself of the sharp images of the death.

Tomorrow, he'd take up Vince's trail and track that murdering bastard to Central America if that was what it took to bring him to justice.

Chapter 14

Longarm awoke in a hotel room the next morning with a slight hangover but a clear purpose in mind. He was going to telegraph Billy Vail and ask for some additional travel money, and then, if Vince had gone on the run, he'd outfit himself for a manhunt.

He shaved, dressed and went downstairs looking for coffee and a decent breakfast. "Where's a good place in Tombstone to eat?" he asked, waking the sleeping desk clerk.

"Copper Kettle is the best," the man said. "Strong coffee and sourdough pancakes. It's just four doors up the street."

"Thanks," Longarm replied, checking his gun and heading outside.

Marshal Yates must have been waiting for him, because the man crossed the street with a grim expression on his face and intercepted Longarm before he could reach the restaurant. "Have you got a few minutes to talk?" Yates asked.

"Sure. As long as it's over coffee and flapjacks."

Yates nodded in agreement, and they went into the restaurant and ordered the same breakfast. After the coffee was poured, and they were alone for a few minutes, Yates leaned forward across the table and asked, "Why didn't you come and tell me last night about what happened to Donita?"

"I went by your office, and it was closed. I didn't know where you live, and I figured that you'd get the news soon enough. This is a small town, and it isn't every day that the bodies of two young women show up at the undertaker's office."

"You should have told me yourself," Yates complained. "It was nearly midnight by the time I learned about Donita being murdered in that shack. By all accounts, I should have looked you up and demanded to know the details."

"That would have been a mistake," Longarm told the lawman.

"You don't show the locals much respect, do you?"

"If they deserve it, I do."

Yates flushed with anger. "You have no right to talk down to me. You don't know a thing about this town or what I do or don't do as a sworn officer of the law."

Longarm had to squelch a powerful urge to reach across the table and grab Tom Yates by the throat. Instead, he forced himself to take another sip of strong black coffee before he said, "I know that you and Vince extort people in order to pay for your gambling habits. I know that the good folks in this town want you to leave. What else do I need to know?"

Yates started to say something, then he changed his mind. "Listen," he finally said, "Tombstone will never be a law abiding town. The Earps and the Clantons and McLaurys set the mold of killing and corruption, and that's what the people here have come to expect."

"Wrong!" Longarm thundered, his voice loud enough to turn heads. "What the good folks of any town expect is an honest lawman, and, before I'm finished here, they'll

136

have one if one can be found to replace you and Vince Pendergast."

Yates jumped to his feet, spilling both of their cups of coffee. He was so livid with rage that Longarm's hand went to the derringer he carried in his vest.

"I'm resigning!" Yates yelled, tossing his badge on the table so hard that it bounced up in the air and struck the window. "I'm finished in this town, and, by damned, you can be the law, since that's what you've wanted all along. I quit!"

Yates started to leave, but Longarm threw out his leg and tripped the former marshal to the floor. Before the man could recover, Longarm was up and had a boot planted squarely between Yates's shoulder blades. There wasn't a sound in the room until Longarm said, "If I find that you're part of the murders of William Pendergast or Donita, I will personally see that you hang by the neck in a hangman's noose. Is that clear?"

Yates twisted his head around and glared up at Longarm. "Let me up, and let's step out into the street. We can settle this just like they did in the OK Corral."

"Nope," Longarm said, bending over and removing the man's gun from his holster. "I just decided that I'm going to throw you in jail."

"On what charge?"

"I'll have come up with one by the time we get there," Longarm promised. "Now get up and start walking."

Longarm jailed Tom Yates, and then he enjoyed his breakfast. After that, he sent a request to Denver for additional funds, explaining that he also needed a federal marshal to come and take over the town while he hunted down Vince Pendergast who Longarm was quite sure had not only murdered Donita, but also his own father and his sister's husband.

All in all, Longarm was pleased and felt that it was a

very busy and highly productive morning . . . especially considering he did have a slight hangover.

When he returned to the marshal's office, Tom Yates was having a fit. "I'm going to sue you for everything you own or ever will own!"

"Good luck," Longarm told the caged ex-lawman. "Because when I'm through with you, you'll be talking to your attorney from behind prison bars."

"Dammit, you've got nothing on me."

"Maybe and maybe not. But I'll find something that will send you off to prison for a good many years. Count on it."

Yates cursed and sat down on the rickety jail cot. He ran his fingers through his hair and stared at the floor. Finally, he got up and came over to the bars.

"Listen, Marshal," he began, "I didn't have anything to do with murder."

Longarm was sitting at the man's cluttered desk going through his correspondence and looking for a sample of Vince Pendergast's handwriting that he could compare to the bloody note in his pocket.

"Is that right?"

"It is," Yates insisted. "I might have asked some of the townspeople for a little extra cash each month so that I could give them additional protection, but . . ."

"That's extortion. Ah ha!" Longarm finally discovered a note with Vince's signature. "Here we go."

"What are you doing?"

"Comparing handwriting samples."

"What?"

"Never mind," Longarm told Yates, seeing that the two handwriting samples were a perfect match. "I'm going to see that you and Vince never get out of prison. I might even get you both hanged."

Yates gripped the cell bars until his knuckles turned

white. "I told you that I didn't have anything to do with murder."

"If that's true, then tell me—did Vince kill them all just so he'd inherit the Tombstone Ranch?"

"He . . . he wasn't going to inherit anything," Yates said quietly.

That piece of news caught Longarm's full attention. "So, his father had written him out of his will?"

"Yeah. He'd given everything to Candice and her husband. Vince went crazy when he found out."

"Where is the Pendergast will?"

"It's supposed to be in the bank's vault."

"But it isn't?"

"No. Vince destroyed it."

"How did he get ahold of the will?" Longarm asked.

"He threatened the bank manager's life and that of his family," Yates said, after a long pause. "It wasn't hard to scare the man witless."

"So," Longarm said. "With no will, the courts would give the ranch in equal parts to both heirs . . . Vince and Candice."

"That's right." He then added, "Or to whichever one proved to be the survivor."

A chill passed down Longarm's spine, and he came to his feet. "Vince *would* kill his sister!"

"I don't know about that," Yates said. "He loves her but . . . well, when he has too much to drink . . . he says some things that make even my stomach churn."

Longarm went over to the cell. "I know that Katy Jessup took the poison meant for me, but why did Vince stab Donita to death?"

"She had become suspicious about the deaths of William Pendergast and Candice's late husband. And even though she and Vince were thicker than thieves, she got big plans and started demanding half of the ranch when it fell into Vince's hands."

"So he just solved that little problem with a hunting knife." Longarm reached into his coat pocket and brought out the knife, which he had cleaned and wrapped in a handkerchief. "Do you recognize this murder weapon?"

"It belonged to Vince."

"That's what I thought." Longarm stepped over to the jail cell. "Is Vince going to try and kill his sister?"

"I wouldn't count it out," Yates said. "Especially if he's out there hiding and drinking."

Longarm knew he had better go back to the ranch and try to protect Candice from her own brother. He anticipated that she still wouldn't believe that he was capable of murder, but that wasn't important. What was important was to keep her alive until he either captured or killed Vince.

"Where are you going?" Yates asked when Longarm grabbed a rifle from the rack and the keys from a hook on the wall.

"I'm going out to try and stop Vince from murdering Candice."

"Let me out of here, and I'll go with you."

"Not a chance."

"You don't know Vince! He's a demon when he gets an idea in his head, and the best man with a gun or rifle that I've ever known. He'll kill you if you try to take him by yourself."

"Maybe," Longarm said, making sure that the Winchester was loaded and in good working condition.

"Dammit, if he kills you, he might come back and kill me too!"

Longarm stopped at the door. "Why would he do a thing like that?"

"Because I'm the one that can testify and put a noose around his neck."

"Oh," Longarm said, "I think what you're really trying to do is to put me between yourself and your deputy so that it's certain that one of you will kill me."

"You're wrong. I don't want to go to prison, and I figure, if I help you capture or kill Vince, that will work in my favor when it comes time to face a judge."

"I doubt if it would," Longarm said coldly as he reached for the door. "From my point of view, you're both as guilty as sin."

"Don't leave me here without a gun! Please, don't do this!"

"You'll be fine," Longarm said. "I'll be back by tomorrow. You've got water, and you can stand to miss a meal or two. Besides, you need to get used to being caged."

Marshal Yates unleashed a stream of cuss words but Longarm paid them no attention and slammed the door behind him. He locked it using the marshal's own keys, and then he headed for the livery where the pigeon-toed horse was still waiting to be returned home.

Chapter 15

When Longarm returned to the ranch, Candice was busy making her first Eastern guests feel at home. Longarm waited until Candice could free herself for a few minutes, then he took her aside and told her that Donita had been murdered and that he strongly suspected that Vince was the one who had wielded the killer's knife.

Candice took the news hard and went to her room. Longarm followed and when the door was closed he said, "It looks like your brother was written out of your father's will. I think he killed your father in revenge and then figured that I knew something and tried to kill me but poisoned Katy by mistake."

"I . . . I can't believe he'd have killed Father," she whispered, looking dazed.

"You need to believe it," Longarm told the shaken woman. "And when Donita tried to blackmail him, or at least demand half this ranch for keeping her silence about the murders . . . Vince killed her, too."

"No!" Candice protested. "*I'm* the one that will inherit Tombstone Ranch."

"Not if you're dead."

The implication of his words was chilling and clear.

143

"Listen," he said, taking her into his arms, "I can't even imagine what you must be feeling. And I can't yet prove that Vince killed your father and poisoned Katy, but there's no doubt he murdered Donita, and I think that your life is in grave danger."

"But Vince and I love each other! Yes, we've had our differences, but . . ."

"Candice, I understand that your father's will is missing."

"That's right."

"If it can be found, I think that will solve the mystery. There's something we don't yet understand. Something that Vince knows, and even Donita knew, but we still don't."

"Father told me many times that Tombstone Ranch was going to be left equally to Vince and myself."

"I'm sure he changed his mind and left you sole inheritor of this ranch. There could even be others mentioned in the will that you don't know about."

"Other inheritors?"

Longarm shrugged. "It's a possibility. Was your father married before meeting your mother?"

"Yes, Father had two wives before he met my mother."

"Any children from those marriages?"

"None were ever mentioned." Candice sat down on the bed. "Custis, this is all too much to comprehend. My head is spinning, and I feel so confused."

He sat down beside her. "I don't feel right leaving you here. Will you come with me?"

"Where to?"

"After your brother."

"I can't do that! My guests are already upset about Father's death. What would they think if I suddenly went away? Why, they'd be insulted and never return."

"Better that happen than Vince find you unprotected."

"I'm always well protected by Bob and the other cowboys."

"They ride out in the morning, and you're often here alone."

"Maura and I will be working in the kitchen and on the cottages all day long. Bob and many of the others will be around more now that we need help with our guests. I'm going to be surrounded by my trusted employees, and I'm not going to go running around with you hunting Vince."

Longarm could tell that there was nothing he could say to change the woman's mind. And since he couldn't force her to accompany him, there was nothing to be done but to go hunting for her brother and put an end to this deadly violence.

"Well," he said, "I guess I'd better get back to Tombstone. I locked Tom Yates up in his own jail cell."

"You what?"

"It's a long story and not a nice one. But the short of it is that Yates has resigned, and I've telegraphed the federal office to let them know that Tombstone needs a new marshal. I expect that someone is being sent to fill in until the town can find an honest replacement."

"Custis, you look exhausted."

"Actually, I'm feeling much better. My lungs feel clear, and I'm just a bit tired."

"You need a good dinner and a long night's sleep."

He supposed that was true. "I don't feel like going back to the cottage where Katy was poisoned."

"Then sleep here with me tonight," Candice said, hugging his waist. "I'm feeling very afraid and confused right now, and I need you."

"Wouldn't that look bad to your wealthy and high-toned guests?"

"They don't have to know you spent the night in my bedroom. Really, Custis, I'll have Maura make you something wonderful and bring it up here this evening. You can have supper in bed, and I'll join you the moment I can get free."

"That sure sounds better than my sleeping alone in a fleabag hotel room in Tombstone," Longarm answered. "But I have to get back to town first thing tomorrow morning and figure out what I'm going to do with Tom Yates. If it were up to me, I'd let him starve in jail for a week or two. But I suppose that wouldn't go over too well with some people."

"I don't care about Yates," she said. "I only care about you, myself and the loyal people that work here at the ranch."

"Nothing wrong with that."

"Then you'll stay tonight?"

"Sure."

Candice brightened. "Good! I'll send Maura up with hot water for a bath. You can borrow my father's pajamas and shaving things and . . ."

"Whoa! In the first place, I doubt that I could fit into your father's clothes because I'm quite a bit larger than he was."

"Well, then, just shave, and I'll see if Maura can wash up some of your things."

Longarm rubbed the stubble on his cheeks. "I guess I could use a little cleaning up, huh?"

"Yes," she told him. "Please don't feel offended . . . but you smell worse than awful."

He had to laugh until he realized that perhaps he carried the scent of death on his person from handling two corpses in less than two days.

"All right. I'll clean up and wait for you."

She glanced at a clock on her dresser. "It's four o'clock, and I won't be able to get away from the guests until about eight. But then I'll hurry upstairs, and we can eat together."

Longarm thought that sounded like a fine idea, and as

146

soon as Candice left him, he kicked off his boots and most of his clothing, then stretched out on the bed and took an afternoon nap.

He was awakened by a firm knock on his door and sat up, his hand instinctively reaching for his six-gun. "Who is it?"

"It's Maura. Your bath is ready next door."

"Thanks."

"I'll put fresh towels right here in the hallway for you, Marshal Long."

"Thanks, again."

He heard her receding footsteps in the hallway and went to open his door. Sure enough, two thick white bath towels, a shaving mug, a razor and a bar of soap were waiting for his pleasure.

Longarm shaved first, and although he wished he'd had a strop to sharpen the razor, he did just fine. Afterward, he took his time in the bathtub and used a scrub brush to work over his hands and fingernails. And finally, he went back to Candy's room and climbed into her bed. He was about to drift off to sleep when the familiar knock sounded at the door.

"Marshal Long?"

"Yeah?"

"Miss Pendergast instructed me to collect your clothing."

"Come on in."

Maura stepped into the bedroom and glanced around. When she saw Longarm in her mistress's bed, she took a little back step, then squared her shoulders and came forward.

"Your clothes, sir?"

Longarm was wearing only his undershorts, but he didn't think much about that as he swung his long legs out of the bed and gathered up his pants, shirt vest and coat. Only when he handed them to the Irish woman did he realize that she might be shocked by this situation. However, he decided not to embarrass her further, and so he just passed the bundle to her, saying, "They're pretty dirty, but take it easy on the vest and coat. I don't have anything to replace them, and I'm low on funds."

"I understand," Maura replied, wrinkling her nose with distaste.

"Listen, my gut is grinding on empty, so could you bring up something to hold me over until Candice and I have supper together up here later this evening?"

There was a pause, then, "And what is it that you'd be wanting to eat at this unusual hour?"

"Well," he said, "a couple of cold beef ribs and a glass of whiskey sounds good."

The Irish woman's eyebrows lifted. "Whiskey and beef ribs?"

"Or pork or a slab of ham. You know. Whatever is handy."

"I'll find something and bring it up at once."

"Thanks. Sorry to trouble you. I guess with the guests starting to arrive, you're going to be real busy for a while."

"I am."

Longarm started to say more, but Maura backed out of the room with his clothes and slammed the door hard enough to rattle the bedroom windows. "That one," Longarm mused to himself, "is deep water."

Maura reappeared about a half hour later with a tray of cold beef, sliced bread and a small glass of whiskey. She sat the tray on the bedside table and turned to leave.

"Say," Longarm called, "I was wondering . . . have you worked for Miss Pendergast a long time?"

She turned. "About five years."

"Then you must like it here."

"It's not at all like Ireland, but it's fine."

The woman did not have an accent but Longarm figured that Maura must have lived in Ireland or she wouldn't have compared the Emerald Isle with Arizona. "Were you born there?"

"Aye."

"How old were you when you came to the United States?"

"Just a baby."

"I see. But you remember Ireland?"

"I didn't say that."

Longarm was momentarily confused. "But you said that Arizona wasn't like Ireland. So, if you don't remember anything about Ireland, how would you know that?"

Maura raised her chin and gave him a look of disgust. "Sir, everyone knows that Ireland is green and that Arizona is brown. Is there anything else that you'd be wanting? If not, I have to attend to my kitchen duties."

"No," he said, "I'm fine.

Maura left again, slamming the bedroom door. Longarm decided that he didn't like the woman and that the feeling was mutual. *Oh, well, you can't charm them all.* He dug into the food she'd brought, and he sipped on the fine whiskey. After that, he climbed back in bed and dozed.

The sun was long gone by the time Candice finally appeared with Maura in tow, both of them carrying trays of steaming food. Candice laid them down on the bed and said, "Maura tells me that you have quite an appetite."

"I do," he agreed. "Now that I'm feeling better, I can't seem to get enough to eat."

"We brought enough up this evening to feed a half dozen people." She turned toward Maura. "You'd better go down and finish up in the kitchen."

"Aye."

When Maura was gone, Longarm said, "She's not very friendly."

"She isn't?"

"Either that, or she's taken a strong dislike to me."

"Did Maura say anything wrong?"

Longarm shook his head. "Nope."

"Well then?"

"It's just that she leaves little doubt that she disapproves of me being here in your bed."

"Maura is a bit of a prude," Candice told him. "If you want, I'll have a word with her about . . ."

"No," he said. "Let's not stir up any more troubles. Let's eat."

"Yes, let's," Candice agreed.

They ate well, and afterward Candice came to bed and lay in his arms until the moon appeared through the open window. Then she turned toward Longarm and kissed his face, his neck, his chest and his lips. "Too bad you're so unwell," she whispered.

"I'm feeling better every minute."

"Well enough to . . . you know."

"To take this a step farther?"

"Yes," she told him as her hands slipped down his long, muscular frame.

Longarm took his time removing her clothes and then he licked her nipples until they were as hard as cold drops of sweet chocolate. When Candice spread her legs, Longarm eased into her very slowly until his thick shaft was buried to the hilt.

"Oh, you feel good!" Candice cried, hugging him tightly.

"So do you."

"Can we just take our time and make this last for an hour?"

"I don't know," he replied. "That sort of depends on you."

She sighed. "I just want to lie here feeling you inside of me for a while."

"That's a tall order, but I'll do my best to fill it."

"You're filling me just fine," she told him. "I wish that we had met under different circumstances."

"Me, too."

"I wish that we had met," she continued, "with my father alive so that he could give my hand away to you in marriage. And that none of these terrible things had happened and that Donita was still alive and Mrs. Jessup and . . ."

"You talk and worry way too much," he said. "Just be silent and let the feelings of what we have right now take over."

"Yes. I will." Candice closed her eyes, and when Longarm began to move inside of her, she moaned with intense pleasure. "That's just perfect."

"Are you thinking about it and not about the past or the future?"

"I am!"

"Good," Longarm said with satisfaction.

He continued his slow, even strokes for almost a half hour until his toes began to tingle, and Candice's fine body was straining upward. Then, he began to move into and out of her faster and harder. When Candice wrapped her long legs around his waist and began to buck and squeal like a mare in heat, Longarm really got serious about the lovemaking. He managed to stretch their pleasure out for another five or ten minutes, and then they both lost control of their bodies.

Candice cried out in ecstasy, and Longarm groaned as he filled her with his seed. When their bodies finally came to rest, they lay perspiring and panting in each other's arms.

"Feel better now?" he asked.

"Oh yes," she said in a low, husky voice. "That is exactly what I needed tonight."

"So did I."

"But you're still going after my brother tomorrow?"

"You know that I must. He's killed too many people already. He might have returned to Tombstone. But, if not, do you have any idea where I might start looking?"

"He has some Mexican friends named Escobar that live just south of the border close to a little village called Naco."

"Have you been there?"

"Yes. Once my father and I went down to Mexico with Vince to buy some Mexican horses. But the horses were all scrubs . . . too small for ranch work. Vince spent most of the time drinking and gambling while we waited, supposedly for his friends to find bigger horses. After a long, hot week, Father and I gave up and came back here. Vince didn't show up for another month, and when he did, he was driving three of the nicest horses you'd ever want to own."

"I take it they were very different from the Mexican ponies."

"Yes, very different. Father paid Vince fifty dollars each for those fine mounts. I learned much later that they had been stolen from an American cattleman who lived over near Douglas. For some reason, he'd never branded the animals."

"Did your father learn of the deception?"

"No," Candice replied. "If he had, he'd have tried to horsewhip Vince. I sent the Douglas cattleman one hundred and fifty dollars, but I never said who I was for fear the man would come here and demand the horses be returned or that Vince be arrested."

Longarm sat up in bed. "Do Vince's friends live right in Naco?"

"No. About two miles to the south of it. But you'd

better not go there because they are a tough bunch. If they discover you're a federal officer of the United States, you won't come back alive."

"Then I'll just have to keep that a secret."

"But . . ."

He placed his forefinger on her lips. "Candice, I'll survive. I speak a little Spanish, and I've crossed the border before after outlaws. It's not legal, and I don't put it in my reports, but sometimes it has to be done in the name of justice."

"Vince would never come back alive. He'll first fight you to the death."

"I know."

Candice hugged him tightly. "Let's just hold each other until we fall asleep and not talk about death and fighting anymore. All right?"

"Sure," he said. "And, if you wake up in the middle of the night and feel like making love again, don't hesitate to wake me."

"You *are* feeling much better."

Longarm took a deep breath, and it didn't hurt like it had when he'd first arrived. "Yes," he agreed, stifling a yawn, "and it's about time."

Chapter 16

Longarm awoke at dawn feeling good. He dressed quietly
while Candy still slept, and then he tiptoed downstairs to
the kitchen where Maura was already up and preparing
breakfast.

"I smell coffee," he said.

"Go away. Nothing is ready."

"That's fine. I'll make my preparations to leave and
come in for some coffee and breakfast before I go."

She glanced around at him. "Did you have good night?"

Longarm didn't know what she meant, but he played it
straight saying, "A *great* night. And how about you?"

"I slept."

He studied her as she bustled around the kitchen. "Is
there some particular reason that you don't like me?
Maybe something I've done or said that has you convinced I'm a no account?"

Her hands were in a bowl of flour dough that she was
preparing for biscuits. Maura looked up at him and said,
"You're here to get this ranch. You think you can marry
Miss Pendergast and have a fine situation for yourself.
But you're wrong!"

Longarm was taken aback by the passion in her voice.

"Why Maura," he said, forcing a smile. "Why are you so concerned about what happens to this ranch? Is it because of your job? Well, if that's the case, then I'll put your mind at ease. If I were to marry Candy, I wouldn't dream of having you fired."

"I don't want to talk to you. Go away."

Longarm shook his head. "You're a strange one, that's for sure. I haven't figured you out."

"And you never will," the Irish woman snapped. "But I have you figured out. I can see right through your act."

"Is that a fact?"

"Aye! And you'll not get away with it!"

Longarm had an answer on the tip of his tongue, but decided to let it die unspoken. "Have a good day, Maura. I'll see you when I return from Old Mexico."

The woman looked up quickly from her work, and Longarm swore that she called him a name that would have made his mother blush. But then she went back to kneading her dough, and Longarm headed out the door. He had to catch and saddle Baldy and then pack a few provisions for the hunt. And while it was true that Vince might be waiting to gun him down in Tombstone, Longarm had a hunch that the killer had fled the country.

It was still early when he returned to Tombstone and unlocked the marshal's office. Tom Yates was pacing back and forth in his cell, and when he saw Longarm, he shouted, "Dammit, you can't hold me in here without a reason."

"I suppose that's true, but I could think of something."

"I want out of here or I demand to have a lawyer sent over from Tucson. There's a fellow over there named James McAndrews. Send him a telegram!"

Longarm didn't appreciate being ordered around. "Sorry, but I'm a bit low on funds."

Yates stuffed his hands deep into his pockets and dragged out a wad of bills. "Here!" he yelled, throwing them between the bars to flutter to the dirty wooden floor. "Take that, and send the telegram now."

Longarm collected the money and counted it. "Thanks," he said. "I can use a few extra bucks for the trip I'm taking to Mexico."

Yates gripped the bars. "Why are you going down there? You need to let me out of this jail."

"Relax. I'm going to pay someone to bring you food and water. And I won't be in Naco more than a few hours."

"You're going to Naco?"

"That's right. Candice told me that's the most likely place to find Vince."

Yates shook his head as if he were having a bad dream. "What if you're killed down there? What about me?"

"I expect that they'll let you out one of these days. Maybe even tomorrow. Anyway, that's not my biggest concern."

"It ought to be because when I get my attorney, I'll make sure that you never have another dime!"

Longarm put Yates's money into his coat pocket and headed for Mexico.

The trip south to the border went well, although Longarm did not see the track of the pigeon-toed horse he figured Vince was riding. He passed through the thriving mining town of Bisbee pushing his borrowed gelding hard. He crossed into Mexico, and when he neared the town of Naco, Longarm could feel the suspicious stares of the Mexicans who saw him riding south in pursuit of a murderer. They did not speak to the tall, tough looking American or nod their heads in greeting or in friendliness. Maybe that was because Longarm looked so grim and formidable. Or maybe it was because so many other tough gringos had ridden south in search of adventure but had instead found violence and death.

157

Naco was easy to find, and it was even less impressive than Longarm had expected. Just a couple of cantinas, some adobe huts and a lot of dogs, kids, chickens and goats wandering around looking dazed and defeated in the dust and the heat. Longarm stopped and bought a half dozen corn tortillas stuffed with spicy beef from an old woman who was cooking them on a rock stove under a brush-covered ramada. She sold him a bottle of warm beer to wash them down, and he paid her twice her asking price . . . one American dollar. When she beamed and showed how happy she was to have the extra money, he asked, "Escobar, señora?"

Her toothless smile evaporated, and she turned away pretending to be suddenly very busy. Longarm looked around and realized that they were being watched by the villagers. He slipped another dollar out of his pocket and softly said, "*Por favor*, señora? Escobar?"

The dollar did the trick, and she somehow managed to point him in the right direction as she tossed the tortillas over the hot stone griddle she used for cooking. Longarm thanked the woman, mounted his horse and rode out of Naco. From Tom Yates's office, he'd confiscated a good Winchester rifle and a double-barreled shotgun in addition to three pistols, which he'd stuffed under his belt. Those weapons, in addition to his usual armament, made him look like a human arsenal.

Longarm didn't care. His plan was simply to ride up to the Escobar place and politely inquire as to the whereabouts of Vince Pendergast. If Vince was present, he'd confront the man and try to arrest him without bloodshed. Failing that, he'd gun the man down—if he could. And, if Vince wasn't at the Escobar place, well, Longarm figured he'd just ride back across the border and start asking questions until he got a new lead on the killer.

The Escobar place was the only one in the general direction that Candice and the old Mexican woman had told him about. This was a hard, dry land mostly covered with sage and creosote bush. Longarm spotted an adobe hacienda off in the distance ringed by cottonwoods. He passed small bunches of skinny cattle and horses all wearing a dozen different brands.

I'll just bet every last one of them has been rustled and driven across the border, he said to himself.

Longarm confirmed his suspicion that the Escobar family's primary source of income was from stealing livestock and driving them across the border. When the Mexicans saw him, they bunched up like their stolen livestock and stood in a tight knot in front of their hacienda.

"Baldy, if Vince is here, this could turn real ugly," he told his gelding. "And, if we have to make a run for it, you'd better have some life left in your legs. At least enough to get us back into the United States. If I get killed, and they take ownership of you, your life is going to take a serious turn for the worse. If you doubt that, look at the sad shape of their skinny horses."

Longarm rode up a through the brush following a narrow wagon track. As he drew nearer, he counted seven armed Mexicans, and all of them looked like seasoned banditos. They were wearing pistols, and one held a shotgun much like the one that Longarm had resting across the fork of his saddle.

"Hombres!" Longarm called, keeping his finger on the trigger of the shotgun and wearing a frozen smile on his cracked lips.

They didn't say a word. Longarm reined his mount to a standstill less than fifty feet from the adobe hacienda. His eyes took in his surroundings, and he saw the shadow of a man with a rifle standing just inside the doorway. Was it Vince standing there ready to potshot him from the saddle?

If the shooting starts, he thought, *I will kill that one first and then the man holding the shotgun. If I'm still alive, I'll go for the rest of them on the run.*

"I am looking for my old amigo, Vince Pendergast!"

The leader of the bunch was a dark, heavyset man with a big paunch that protruded over his belt. He wore a pistol on his right hip and a dagger on his left hip, in addition to a knife whose bone handle Longarm could see protruding from his boot top. One of his ears was missing, and, in the other, he wore a gold earring.

He glared at Longarm, and then he made a quick, slashing motion with his hand and gave an order that Longarm did not understand, but guessed to mean that he was supposed to dismount.

Longarm knew that if he got off his horse, he was finished. "No," he said, shaking his head and then pointing to the hacienda. "I need to see Vince Pendergast, my amigo."

The big Mexican turned to the hacienda and shouted an order. Suddenly, Vince burst out into the sunlight with the rifle sweeping upward. Longarm spurred Baldy hard and, in the same instant, raised the shotgun and fired both barrels at Vince. Luckily, the blast struck Vince in the face and neck, beheading and slamming his bloody corpse into the wall of the hacienda.

The other Mexicans would have drawn their weapons and opened fire except that Longarm had tossed his shotgun aside and now had his pistol trained on the leader.

"No, señor!" he shouted in a warning that left no room for misinterpretation.

For a moment, Longarm thought they were all going to act crazy and kill him, but the heavyset man, seeing his own death stamped all over Longarm's rugged and determined expression, cried out for his men to freeze.

"Gracias," Longarm said, eyes flicking to Vince whose headless body was quivering, scratching and kicking mindlessly at the dirt while spouting a pulsing gush of blood.

Longarm kept his gun trained on the leader as he began to back the gelding away. He backed poor Baldy almost a hundred yards, and then he spun the animal around and spurred him hard. Back north they ran, scattering the stolen bands of thin horses and tick-infested cattle. Longarm glanced over his shoulder and saw the Mexicans scrambling to get to their horses and give chase.

"Come on, Baldy!" he shouted. "We're only a couple of miles from the border!"

Baldy laid back his ears and ran like a demon. Several times the buckskin almost took a spill as it raced headlong through the dense scrub brush, but it managed to keep going. When the gallant horse finally began to falter and show signs of collapse, Longarm drew it down to a walk and twisted around in his saddle. The Mexicans were still coming, but they were at least a mile off.

"Baldy," Longarm said, "do you think we can make it a while longer?"

The good horse was blowing hard, heavily lathered and dripping sweat. But it seemed to understand that its fate, as well as that of its rider, depended on speed, so it broke into a weary trot. Longarm wondered if they would reach and pass the border before they were overtaken. He suspected not.

Twisting around in his saddle again, he judged the speed of his pursuers and knew that they would overtake him before the sun went down. Longarm searched for high ground where he could make a stand until darkness when his horse recovered. But there was no high ground— only a pile of rocks and brush. He figured that would have to do and reined Baldy toward them, urging the horse into a lumbering gallop. When he reached the cover, Longarm jumped off his played out mount, dragged it into cover and then slipped his Winchester out of his saddle scabbard.

He was fortunate the sun was at his back, and, therefore,

directly in the faces of his pursuers. Low and gleaming like a fiery-eyed cyclops, it was blinding, and when the Mexicans foolishly rode into Longarm's rifle range, he opened fire with methodical, deadly effect. Before the Escobar men could retreat, he emptied three of their saddles.

Longarm waited to see if they would regroup and attack again in the last moments before the sun died. They did not, and as darkness fell upon the hard, killing land, he remounted Baldy and headed for Tombstone. What he had done had been far outside of his legal authority as a sworn federal officer. But, if he had not killed Vince, the man would have killed Candice and perhaps even himself in a second ambush.

Longarm rode his horse back into Bisbee about midnight. He roused the livery man and made sure that Baldy was grained and rubbed down and put away with plenty of hay and clean water.

"Mister," the sleepy-eyed livery man said when Longarm started to walk away, "you sure used this horse hard."

"I know, and for that I'm sorry. But it was necessary."

"That's what everyone says. But there's never no excuse for abusing a good animal."

"You're right," Longarm told the man as he trudged wearily up the street toward the nearest hotel.

Chapter 17

Longarm awoke the next morning and went to the livery to claim his horse and ride on to Tombstone, but Baldy had gone lame in the right front foot.

"What's wrong with him?"

"He threw a shoe and bruised his frog," the livery man answered.

"Can he be ridden today?"

"Only if you put another shoe with a protective leather pad on him and stay out of rough country."

Longarm had a look at Baldy's hoof, and he could see that the horse had, indeed, rock bruised the soft center of his foot. "How long will it take the blacksmith to take care of my horse?"

"He's out at the Baily Ranch shoeing horses all day. I expect that he could shoe your horse the first thing tomorrow morning."

Longarm wasn't pleased. If he had been the owner of the buckskin gelding, he'd probably have dickered for a sound horse in exchange, but since Baldy belonged to the Tombstone Ranch, he decided he had better just rest both the horse and himself for a day and then proceed north in the morning. Besides that, he needed a little time to think about what had happened since he'd been in Arizona, and what role he still had left to play with Candice and the Tombstone Ranch.

So he went back to the hotel and spent the day napping and enjoying his ease. If he'd had more money, he would have bought a new coat and hat that he saw in a storefront window. But he was low on funds and had used the last of his cash to eat and drink well. Tomorrow, he'd return to Tombstone, and, unless Billy Vail had failed him, Longarm expected there would be additional funds waiting for him, wired directly from Denver.

He slept well that night, and it was nearly noon the following morning when the blacksmith finally got around to working on Baldy. It took the man an hour to do the necessary corrective shoeing.

"This is too good a horse to have been hard used," the burly blacksmith said, casting a hard stare of disapproval toward Longarm. "You had better take it easy, or he'll go lame again. These bad rock bruises can take weeks to heal completely."

"I'm only going to the Tombstone Ranch."

"I knew old William Pendergast," the blacksmith said. "How is his daughter doing since her husband died suddenly?"

"She's doing all right," Longarm answered, not wanting to get into any specifics.

"That family has had a lot of hard luck. I heard that one of their maids got poisoned."

"Yeah," Longarm said, "I heard the same thing."

The blacksmith wiped his sweaty brow on the back of his dirty and muscular forearm. "They're a good family except for Vince. He's the bad apple of the lot."

"Well," Longarm said, "I have a feeling that Vince isn't going to be causing anyone any more trouble."

"That'd be a blessing," the blacksmith said. "Be a dollar and two bits, mister."

Longarm paid the man and was soon on the road north. It was only about twenty-five miles to Tombstone, and the road was clear and well traveled. He didn't push Baldy for fear that the gelding would go lame again. When he arrived in Tombstone, he rode straight up to the marshal's office and was met by a crowd of agitated people.

"What's going on?" he asked one of the men standing near the open front door.

"Someone killed Marshal Tom Yates a few hours ago."

Longarm's jaw almost dropped to his feet. "That's . . . are you sure?"

"Yep. Say, you're the federal lawman, ain't you?"

"That's right. I put Yates in jail."

"Well," the man said, "you should have locked the front door because someone must have come in there this morning and carved Tom up like a Thanksgiving turkey."

Longarm tied Baldy and pushed through the crowd. When he got inside, several men were just about to carry Yates out on a stretcher. Longarm took one look at the former marshal of Tombstone and knew that Yates had met a terrible death. He grabbed the body by the arm and, sure enough, Yates hadn't been dead more than an hour or two.

"Marshal, who do you think did this to Tom?" one of the men asked, looking a little green around the gills from the sight he'd just witnessed.

"I have no idea," Longarm muttered, telling the man the truth. He would have blamed Yates's death on Vince, but since he'd killed Vince the day before, it was obvious that someone else was the murderer.

But who?

"Marshal, is it okay to take him over to the undertaker's office?" one of the men asked.

"Sure."

Longarm waited until the body was carried outside, and then he closed the door to the office and carefully examined the jail cell looking for some clue as to the killer's identity. But he didn't find a thing that would help. And, from the looks of Yates, the killer had been a man, because no woman could have delivered that kind of terrible carnage. Maybe it was even someone that Yates had trusted and allowed to momentarily catch him off guard. Whoever had stabbed Yates to death had been tough, ruthless and strong.

And just when I thought I had this whole thing wrapped up as neat as a Christmas package, he thought morosely. *Now, I've got still another murderer out there someplace.*

Feeling deflated because he thought the case had ended with Vince's death, Longarm sat down at what had been Vince Pendergast's desk. He propped his feet up and laced his hands behind his head, trying to imagine who he had overlooked in this investigation.

After about twenty minutes, all he knew was that somehow the deaths of Candice's husband, her father, Donita, Katy, Vince and now Tom Yates were interrelated. But what was the relationship? The only one that Longarm could think of was the Tombstone Ranch, and who it would pass on to if Candice were also murdered. That had to be the common bond that every one of the murder victims shared. Tom Yates must have had some information that would have affected the final outcome of the ownership of Tombstone Ranch.

Longarm mused aloud. "What did Yates know that caused him to be murdered in broad daylight in his own jail cell?"

The more Longarm considered the mystery, the more he realized that he had no idea who had murdered everyone. That meant there was nothing to do but to return to the ranch and to try and protect Candice in case she was the next intended victim.

That decision reached, Longarm headed for the door. He would push Baldy a little harder these last few miles, and he hoped that whoever the killer was, he had not gotten to what had to be his last victim—Candice, who *had* to be the final obstacle in the path of his deadly and still unfathomable intentions.

When he arrived at the ranch, Candice was busy helping Maura prepare supper. But when she saw Longarm, she drew him into the parlor where they could speak in private.

"Custis, what happened?"

"I found your brother in Naco, Mexico," he replied. "And I'm sorry, but he opened fire, and I had to kill him."

Candice broke into tears, and Longarm hugged her tightly until she finally regained her composure. "Did he . . . did he admit to killing our father and the others?"

"No," Longarm said. "There wasn't a word spoken between us. The fight happened very fast, and I had to leave on the run."

"Was he with the Escobar gang of banditos?"

"Yes."

Candice shook her head. "Well, I guess that's the end of it."

"Not quite. Someone got into the jail cell and stabbed Tom Yates to death just this morning."

Her shock was almost as pronounced as his had been upon hearing this baffling news. "But who could have done it? And why?"

"I have no idea. Has Maura been out of your sight today?"

"No. Custis, you don't think that she is the one that poisoned Kathy and . . ."

"I don't know what to think," he said. "But someone is killing people, and the only thing that makes any sense to me is that they're doing it to gain control of this ranch."

"But *I* have control of the ranch."

"That's right."

Her eyes widened. "Then you think my life is still in danger? Or do you believe that I'm somehow mixed up in these murders?"

"I don't think you're mixed up in anything except a tangled web that could end your life. That's why I'm sticking close to you from now on."

"I'd like that."

"Good. So I guess I might as well meet your guests."

"Three more families have arrived just in the past couple of days. I'll introduce them all to you this evening."

"And what is my . . . title or status to be? Lover? Protector?"

"How about fiancé?" she asked.

Longarm smiled. "If that's what you want to tell them, then do so. Just don't mention that I'm a federal officer and we're trying to solve some very grisly murders."

"Don't worry, I wouldn't dream of saying that."

"Good."

Longarm had met Candice's distinguished guests, and they were both friendly and impressive. Rich Easterners, they were charming and excellent conversationalists, but really not his kind of folks. So Longarm mostly listened, and, as soon as he could do it without being noticed, he slipped out of their company and headed out to share his free time with the cowboys. They had, of course, learned about the deaths of both Vince and Tom Yates, and they must have been eager to ask Longarm questions, but they were reserved and hardworking men who had learned to mind their own business.

Bob was the leader and foreman. He was a man that led by example, and one who always took on the most difficult jobs. From what Longarm could tell, Bob was well liked and respected by all the hands, but he was a quiet man who rarely spoke his mind unless pressed for an opinion.

Longarm found him an intriguing character, and one evening as they sat out in front of the bunkhouse smoking and talking about the weather, horses and cattle, Longarm suddenly asked, "I was wondering where you grew up. I can usually tell by the way a person talks and uses words, but I confess you've got me stumped."

Bob was slow to answer. Finally, he said, "Oh, I grew up here and there."

"Is that a fact? What did your family do for a living?"

"They ranched. My father was a cowboy like myself. He tried making a go of ranching, but he always failed and had to go back to work for other men."

"Here in Arizona?"

"Sometimes. Other times we lived in Colorado and Texas."

"Colorado, huh?" Longarm said. "What part?"

Bob ground out his cigarette and stared up at the moon. Finally, he said, "The southwest corner."

"Near Durango?"

"Yeah."

"Then you must know the Hanford family. They've got the largest ranch in that part of the state."

"Oh, sure."

"Did your father ever work for the Hanfords?"

"Yeah. We lived there on the ranch for a while."

Bob had been squatting on his boot heels, and now he stood up and said, "Think I'll be going to bed. Got to do a lot of fence repair work in the morning."

"Good night," Longarm said, realizing that he'd been mistaken because the Hanford family ranched in *south-eastern* Colorado near Pueblo. *What had he been thinking? More importantly, what was Bob thinking?*

Longarm was accustomed to people lying to him about their backgrounds once they found out he was a lawman. But he hadn't expected lies from Candice's most trusted cowboy, and that got him to wondering if Bob didn't have something to do with the murders.

"Candice," he said, later that evening, "that Bob is a fine fella. How long has he worked for the ranch?"

"About eight years. And yes, Bob is a fine man, and I've come to rely heavily on his judgment."

"Where is he from?"

"I seem to recall him telling me that he was born and raised near Tucson. The only relative he has ever mentioned practices law over there."

"Do you remember the lawyer's name?"

"No. I don't think that Bob ever mentioned it. Wait a minute. I think he said his cousin's first name was James."

"James Talbot?" Longarm asked, unable to hide his sudden excitement.

"I don't know."

"Candice, didn't you tell me that your brother had a lawyer send you a letter demanding you sell this ranch and split the proceeds?"

"That's right."

"Did you respond to the letter?"

"It was an outrageous demand, and I paid it no mind."

"Did you keep the letter?"

Candice frowned. "Probably."

"Could you look for it right now?"

"Is it really that important?"

"It might well be," Longarm told her. "Let's go see if we can find the letter."

Candice was confused, but she led him into her father's office and opened a file drawer. "I keep things like that under a miscellaneous file."

Longarm waited patiently while she went through the file, and when Candice extracted a letter, he reached for it and saw that the letter was, indeed, from a James A. Talbot.

"You were right," she said. "How could you have guessed that attorney's last name?"

"It was the same one that Tom Yates demanded to have represent him when he was jailed. And here's the best part . . . I have a strong suspicion that this Tucson lawyer, James A. Talbot, is related to your trusted foreman, Bob."

"How odd!"

"Yes," Longarm said, his mind racing, "isn't it? I think we may have found the key that will unlock the mystery of these sudden and unexplained deaths."

"You think Bob is somehow involved?"

"If Maura was with you this morning, do you know where Bob was all morning?"

"Probably out working on our south range fences."

"The ones closest to Tombstone."

"That's right but . . . but surely you don't think he could have killed Yates!"

"I have no other suspects in mind," Longarm said. "But before I question the man, I think I'd better go have a visit with that Tucson attorney. He has to be involved in this somehow."

Candice shook her head. "I don't know what to think. Bob is the one upon whom I've most come to rely and trust since father died."

"I'll be leaving first thing in the morning," Longarm told her. "I'll ride up to Benson and catch the westbound to Tucson. With any luck, I'll be back here in a day . . . two at the most."

"Do you have to leave?"

"If we want to find out who killed Tom Yates, and how his death ties in with the others . . . then yes, I have to go to see that attorney."

"But what could he possibly have to do with any of this?"

"Do you know where your father had his will written?"

Her hand flew to her mouth. "In Tucson!"

"And do you know the name of the attorney he used?"

"No."

Longarm folded the letter and placed it in his inside coat pocket. "If I had any money, I'd bet that your father used James Talbot to write his will . . . or at least to change it, cutting Vince off as one of his heirs."

Candice nodded with slow understanding. "Would he keep a copy of father's will?"

"Of course. And once I find it, we'll know who stands to win this ranch in the event of your sudden and untimely death."

"But why do you think it might be Bob?"

"Why not? He has access to the people that would have been ahead of him as heirs. He's in the perfect position to have orchestrated the murders."

"But how could he have gotten poison into the food that was delivered to you and Katy?"

"Good question," Longarm said. "But the answer won't come until I see that original will."

"What makes you think he'll let you see it?"

Longarm patted his badge. "I have this, and I'll need a letter from you giving me permission to make an exact copy."

"Oh, I wish that I could go with you!"

"I do, too," he said.

"But I can't. Not with the guests here now expecting me to wait on them hand and foot. We've a horseback ride scheduled first thing tomorrow morning. I could ask Bob to do it for me, but the guests would be upset."

Longarm placed his hands on her shoulders. "Can you use a gun?"

"Yes. Father taught me how."

"Then carry one at all times, and when you go to bed tomorrow night, lock your door."

"All right."

"One more thing," Longarm said. "I was expecting

money when I rode into Tombstone. I sent off a telegram to Denver requesting additional travel funds but they never arrived. I'm dead broke."

"I'll give you money," she offered, "but please don't use that word."

"What word?"

"Dead."

Longarm understood, and he made himself a promise that if he missed the train either to or from Tucson, he'd rent a horse and ride hard so that Candice did not have to spend any more time alone than was necessary. In his mind, he already had Bob pegged as the man behind the murders. The only real question left unanswered was if Bob was acting all on his own.

Chapter 18

Longarm got lucky and caught the train out of Benson headed for Tucson the very next afternoon. The train ride was less than fifty miles long so he arrived at the former territorial capital about six that evening, just as the sun was going down.

Tucson was nestled in a high desert valley surrounded by four mountain ranges: the Santa Catalinas to the north, the Rincons to the east, the Santa Ritas to the south and the Tucsons to the west. Longarm had been through this old city many times in the past and knew that it had first been founded in 1700 by the Jesuit priest, Father Kino, when he created the San Xavier Mission at the ancient village of Bac. Tucson had known many masters, first the fierce Apache, then the Spaniards, the Mexicans and, finally, the Americans.

Tucson was the Arizona Territory's largest and most historic city, and Longarm had nothing but praise for its sunny and temperate climate as well as its good Mexican food and beautiful and passionate women. But now, despite the hunger that gnawed at his empty belly, Longarm was a man on a mission, that being to seek out and find the lawyer named James A. Talbot and to see the will that he had drawn for the late William Pendergast.

It wasn't hard to find Talbot's office on Stone Avenue, and, as luck would have it, the attorney happened to be working late and was just about to leave for home when Longarm appeared unannounced and unexpected at his door.

James Talbot was in his fifties, but still trim and quite handsome. Standing about six feet tall, his black hair was long and sprinkled with just enough silver to make him appear very distinguished.

"I'm sorry," the lawyer said, opening his door to address Longarm, "but we're closed, and I'm on my way out for the evening. If you have business, please call again tomorrow morning after ten o'clock."

"I do have business with you," Longarm said, showing the lawyer his badge. "And it can't wait until tomorrow morning."

Talbot's assured smile died on his lips, and he opened the door to let Longarm enter. Striding over to his desk, he stepped behind it as if for protection and asked, "What is the nature of your visit?"

"I've come from the Tombstone Ranch on the behalf of Candice Pendergast. I need to see her father's will, which you drew up prior to his death."

"I'm sorry. That is confidential."

Longarm had expected this reply, and he showed the man the letter that Candice had written authorizing him to see and obtain a copy of the will. Talbot was not pleased.

"Very well," he said with unconcealed reluctance. "You can see Mr. Pendergast's last will and testament tomorrow morning."

"I need to do it right now."

"Impossible."

Talbot went over to the hat rack and got his derby, then started to approach the door, but Longarm blocked his

176

path saying, "You aren't leaving until I see that will."

"Marshal, you are treading on very, very thin legal ice."

"Perhaps," Longarm told him, "but lives are in danger and murders have been committed. So I have no choice but to insist that I have that will right now."

They had a war of wills that lasted nearly a minute, and then Talbot relented and snapped, "All right. You can see the will, but not take possession. I will, however, agree to your receiving a copy in the near future."

"Uh-uh," Longarm grunted. "You could alter the copy and claim that I was lying about the original."

"If that is your position, I must ask you to leave my office."

"You can ask all you want," Longarm said, his voice now hard and flat. "Now, are you going to cooperate or shall I start going through your file cabinets until I find the document?"

"All right!" Talbot shouted in a fit of anger. "But I can assure you there will be legal repercussions for this outrageous action."

"Take a number and get in line behind all the others that have threatened me," Longarm said, matter-of-factly.

Talbot disappeared into another room. Longarm heard the sound of his file drawers opening and then being slammed shut. He went to the door and watched until the lawyer extracted a thick file and began to thumb through it.

"I'll look at the entire file."

"Like hell you will!" Talbot hissed.

Longarm took three strides and grabbed the file from the lawyer's hands a moment before he headed for the exit.

"Hey!" Talbot cried. "You can't take that! Come back here!"

"I'll return it later."

Longarm headed for a cafe where he could take his time

177

examining the file as well as get a good supper. He found a place called the Tucson Skillet, went inside and took an empty table in the back of the room.

"What'll you have?" a man asked as soon as he was seated.

"Coffee. Steak on the rare side. Potatoes. Apple pie or some other kind for dessert. You know, the works."

"Comin' up!"

Longarm opened the file and read the will. It was short and quite straightforward. William Pendergast had left the ranch and most of its property to Candice with one dollar to be paid to Vince lest anyone think he had been left out as an oversight. In the event of Candice's death, the estate was to be left to her husband. What was really interesting was that a third heir had been named in the event that both Candice and her husband were deceased. The recipient was named as Bob Parks, the Tombstone Ranch foreman.

"All right," Longarm said to himself. "But why?"

The answer was found buried deep in the file, in a letter that had been sent by Bob ten years earlier to William Pendergast. In it, Bob had pointed out that since he was the old rancher's illegitimate son, he ought to receive something as an heir—otherwise, he would discredit the old man by showing up and embarrassing his wife and family.

Blackmail.

A copy of the reply that Pendergast had written to Bob included a cowboy job offer, and the promise that he would be named in the will if he conducted himself as a loyal employee and kept their secret. At that time, Pendergast promised that Bob would be fairly rewarded.

"That's it," Longarm said, knowing that Candice's life was in real danger. "Motive for murder."

Longarm quickly ate his supper, paid his bill and went directly to the nearest livery.

"What do you want at this hour?" the crotchety old man who owned the livery snapped with irritation when Longarm interrupted his supper.

"I need to rent a horse."

"Come back in the morning."

"What is it with you Tucson folks? You're the second fella that's told me to come back. I tell you, I need a horse right now!"

"Get lost, bub."

Longarm reached out and balled the man's shirtfront up in his fists. "I'm a United States marshal. I can pay you a couple day's rent tonight . . . or you can hope you'll get paid sometime in the future by some government clerk way off in Denver. Now, which is it to be, mister?"

"I'll take your money."

"Wise decision. I need to leave your horse in Benson and then go on to the Tombstone Ranch, which is just down south of . . ."

"I know where it's at. I knew old man Pendergast. Liked him. What business do you have there?"

"My business is none of your business," Longarm said shortly. "Just get me a fast horse."

"What the hell is the hurry?"

"Move!" Longarm shouted, hoping that he could get to Candice in time.

The old livery man cussed a blue streak, but he moved faster than Longarm had thought him capable, and within thirty minutes he was galloping east, following the railroad tracks and heading back in the direction of Tombstone with William Pendergast's last will and testament tucked deep in his saddlebags.

Chapter 19

The moon was bright, and although he might have cut a little south and saved himself a few miles, Longarm decided to follow the railroad tracks and the accompanying wagon road. His horse was a palomino, a tall, high-headed animal with as rough a gallop as Longarm had ever endured. The angry old livery man had found a way to retaliate against Longarm.

Yet, the palomino was strong, fast and had exceptional endurance. It was also eager to run, and, after a few miles, Longarm had to rein it down to a slower gait knowing that he needed to pace the animal or he would not last the night's journey.

The road back to Benson was all uphill. Longarm had heard the railroad conductor say that the climb was over three thousand feet and the palomino had to work hard. Mile by mile, they hurried on with the land changing, turning to redder rock and greening up more than it had been in the lower Sonoran Desert.

"You're the roughest riding son of a bitch I've ever had the misfortune to ride," Longarm grated sometime after midnight, as he crossed an arroyo and galloped back up the other side, hearing a coyote mournfully howl at the moon.

The palomino threw its head, tossing slobber. Longarm pushed it on toward the Tombstone Ranch. He was wondering if Candice had any idea that Bob was actually her illegitimate half brother. Probably not. There was certainly no resemblance between them.

It was probably five o'clock in the morning when the exhausted palomino trotted into a still sleeping Benson. Longarm didn't even bother to awaken the livery man, but instead unsaddled the horse and transferred his gear onto Baldy, who was now well rested.

"You're going back home," he told the buckskin, tightening Baldy's cinch as he heard a cock crow to greet the rising sun just now peeking over the Dragoon Mountains.

Baldy was sure a lot easier on a man than the Tucson palomino, and, since they didn't have that far to go, Longarm gave the gelding its head and let it tear down the empty road toward Tombstone Ranch. He was dog tired, but all his thoughts were on Candice, and he sure hoped she was alive.

Would Bob still be at the ranch? Surely he must have known that Longarm would be going to Tucson for no other reason than to see Pendergast's attorney. And once that occurred, this deadly game would be over. Maybe the ranch foreman had decided to make a run for freedom. Longarm hoped that was the case rather than that he had committed one more murder.

How would Bob kill Candice if she was already alerted and armed? Poison her?

The closer Longarm got to the ranch, the more he felt that he was missing out on something of critical importance in this case. He had a nagging but strong sense that something just did not quite add up. For one thing, how would a cowboy manage to poison at least three people without help from the Pendergast kitchen?

I'll just bet that Maura is in on this, he told himself about the time he finally crossed onto Tombstone Ranch land. *She just* has *to be!*

The sun was well off the eastern horizon when Longarm rode into the ranch yard, and he knew without asking that he was too late. All the cowboys except for Bob and a good many guests were gathered around the front of the house, and they looked devastated.

"Marshal Long," a young cowboy named Jeb said, "where have you been?"

"I had to go to Tucson. What happened?"

"Miss Pendergast had a bad fall from her horse. Cinch broke, and she's still unconscious. Bob rode for a doctor, but he hasn't returned yet."

"Is Maura inside?"

"Yes, sir. She's with Miss Pendergast. Hasn't left her bedside since the accident happened late yesterday."

Longarm handed his reins to Jeb and took the front porch steps two at a time. He burst into the house, and when he saw no one, he hurried upstairs to Candice's bedroom, hoping that she hadn't already been poisoned to death by Maura.

When he slammed into the bedroom, Maura was leaning over Candice with a glass containing a yellowish liquid.

"Hold it!" Longarm shouted, leaping forward and snatching the glass from her hand.

"What are you doing?" Maura demanded.

Before he answered, Longarm felt Candice's wrist for a pulse. He heaved a visible sigh of relief, and then he turned to the Irish woman. "I'm stopping you from poisoning her."

"What?"

"You heard me."

Maura's eyes burned with hatred. "You're out of your mind!"

"Am I?" Longarm pushed the glass of liquid toward the housekeeper and cook. "If so, then *you* drink this."

Maura's reaction was to jump backward, hands instinctively reaching for her throat.

"Yeah," Longarm said with a cold smile, "you've poisoned Mr. Pendergast and Candice's late husband, and then you got Katy instead of me. Go ahead and drink the poison, Maura. Either that, or face a hangman."

Her hate-filled eyes brimmed with tears born of rage and defeat. "Go to hell!"

"If I do, you'll be there waiting for me," he said, placing the glass on a nightstand. "Why did you help Bob?"

"I don't know what you're talking about."

Longarm moved over to Candice's bedside. One side of her face was purplish and covered with a nasty looking scab. But her pulse was strong, and the woman's breathing deep and steady. Longarm peeled the covers back and examined Candice for broken bones. He saw that her arm was splinted.

"Did you splint the arm?"

"No. One of the guests did with the help of a cowboy."

Longarm shook his head. "I expect that Bob said that after he inherited this ranch, he'd marry you."

Maura said nothing, and, needing a confession, Longarm fed her a lie. "But Bob was already married. He has a wife in Tucson."

"Liar!" she exploded, fists clenched.

"I met her just yesterday. Nice woman, but just as naive as yourself. Bob has two kids, but then, I don't suppose he told you about them. Let's see, Little Bob is seven now and . . ."

Maura snapped. "That bloody bastard said he loved me,

184

and we'd have this ranch together if I helped him and Marshal Yates!"

"Well," Longarm said, "Bob murdered Yates in his own jail cell because he didn't want to share his inheritance with him . . . or you. Sorry about that," Longarm said, not feeling a bit sorry. "But the only thing you're going to get is a hangman's noose."

Maura's whole body shook as if an invisible hand from above had just reached down and seized her by the throat. Then, she grabbed the glass of yellow liquid, and, before Longarm could tear it away, she swallowed it all down.

"You fool!" he raged. "You might have got off with a lifetime prison sentence."

"Aye, but what kind of life would that have been?" Maura gasped, lurching toward the door.

He grabbed and spun her around. "Where is Bob now?"

"In Tombstone."

Maura choked and collapsed to her knees. She began to convulse, and, as Longarm stood and watched, her face contorted into a terrible grimace. Then she died, thrashing around on the carpet.

Longarm spent the rest of that day at Candice's bedside. Sometimes he dozed off and was awakened by an anxious cowboy or one of the Eastern guests. Just before sunset, Candice regained consciousness, and he held her close and told her about Maura and Bob and her father's secret will that he'd obtained in Tucson.

"So, it's over at last," Candice whispered, looking pale and drawn.

"Not quite. There's still Bob. He's probably waiting for one of the cowboys to ride into Tombstone and tell everyone that you are dead."

She shuddered. "And then what would he do?"

"Come back here and tell everyone that he couldn't find a doctor. Probably spend a few days pretending to grieve

185

and then head for Tucson to retrieve your father's last will and testament."

"They had it so well planned."

"Yes," Longarm agreed. "They poisoned everyone that counted as an heir to this ranch except for yourself."

"And Maura would have done that if it hadn't been for you. I don't know why my cinch broke. I. . . ."

Longarm touched her cheek. "You're not thinking quite clearly. I would be willing to bet that Bob cut the cinch almost through knowing it would break at a gallop."

"Yes. I suppose that he must have." She took a deep breath. "I can't bear the idea of you leaving me so soon. But are you going to Tombstone to arrest Bob now?"

"I'm tired of riding," Longarm confessed. "Let's send one of your cowboys to town with the story, and then let Bob race back here with the sad tale of how he couldn't find a doctor in time."

Candice squeezed his hand. "Good idea, my darling."

Longarm took Jeb aside and told him what to tell the people in Tombstone. Told him how to act as if Miss Pendergast were already dead.

"I'll do it, Marshal, but I sure don't understand. You just told us that she was going to be fine."

"I'll explain later. Just do what I say."

"Yes, sir."

Three hours later, Bob came racing into the ranch yard. Longarm was waiting with Candice up in her room, and they both heard Bob thunder up the stairs. When he burst into the bedroom and saw Longarm with a gun pointed at his heart and Candice with a pale, accusing smile on her lips, he started to turn and run.

"Hold it!" Longarm shouted.

Bob must have known he'd hang because he raced down the stairs and out into the yard. The other cowboys were dumbstruck as he untied his winded horse and tried to mount up and ride as if Satan himself was on his heels.

"Stop or I'll shoot!" Longarm bellowed as he stepped down from the porch with his Colt in his hand.

Bob had no intention of stopping so that he could be arrested, tried and hanged. He drove his spurs into his horse and reined it away hard.

Longarm shot him the first time in the chest and finished him off with a second slug that blew off his hat and the back of his skull. Then, he said to the astonished collection of cowboys and refined Easterners, "Bob and Maura murdered Mr. Pendergast, Candice's husband and poor Katy Jessup. Maura is dead upstairs. Take her and Bob's bodies to town and tell the undertaker to give them paupers' funerals in the worst burial plots in the whole damn cemetery."

They were too stunned right then to ask questions, but instead, simply watched as Longarm went back inside, climbed the stairs and wrapped Candice Pendergast in his strong arms.

Watch for

LONGARM AND THE DRUID SISTERS

286th novel in the exciting LONGARM series
from Jove

Coming in September!